Saving Mr. Bingle

Sean Patrick Doles

New Orleans Stories
New Orleans/Austin

This is a work of fiction. Names, characters, places, and incidents
are either the product of the author's imagination or are used
fictitiously, and any resemblance to actual persons, living or dead,
business establishments, events, or locales is entirely coincidental.

Mr. Bingle is a registered trademark of Dillard's Inc. This book is
not affiliated with or authorized by Dillard's Inc.

PRINTED IN THE UNITED STATES OF AMERICA

Visit our website at www.savingmrbingle.com.

Book cover designed with assistance from Casey Williamson.
New Orleans Stories and its logo, the letters N and O stacked
vertically, are trademarks of New Orleans Stories. Photo detail of
Mr. Bingle on front cover courtesy of The Historic New Orleans
Collection.

New Orleans Stories
7301 Burnet Rd., Ste. 102, PMB 107
Austin, TX 78757

First New Orleans Stories paperback printing: September, 2004
Library of Congress Control Number: 2004112237

ISBN 0-9758996-0-0

1 3 5 7 9 10 8 6 4 2

*"The first time I performed with Mr. Bingle
at the Crippled Children's Hospital, I placed
his hand on the knee of a little boy whose hands
were twisted into little claws. That boy slowly
straightened one of his hands and laid it
down on Bingle's. That's when I knew
what I'd been sent here to do."*

Edwin H. "Oscar" Isentrout,
Puppeteer & Voice of Mr. Bingle

*A portion of the proceeds from the sale
of* Saving Mr. Bingle *will be donated to the
Edwin H. "Oscar" Isentrout Memorial Fund
to purchase a tombstone for the unmarked
grave of Edwin H. "Oscar" Isentrout. Visit
www.savingmrbingle.com to learn more.*

For Mom & Pop

You taught me that I could fly,
You gave me room to spread my wings,
You picked me up when I fell,
You gave me courage to try again.

Prologue

Once upon a time...

NEW ORLEANS – Fillmore's Department Stores Inc., one of the nation's largest department-store chains, has announced its purchase of New Orleans-based Marigny Brothers Department Stores Inc. for $80.94 million, cementing its hold on the South and Midwest. Based in Dallas, Texas, Fillmore's operates 272 stores throughout the country, while Marigny Brothers has 10 stores throughout Louisiana, Mississippi, and Florida, including four stores in Metro New Orleans.

The purchase is the biggest yet for Fillmore's Chairman Willard Fillmore I, who has focused on expanding through a series of small acquisitions over the past decade. Both chains target mid- to upper-income customers in many of the same medium-sized markets. The move will help the retailer cut costs by consolidating advertising, management, and distribution.

Store officials Monday declined to comment on the future of any of its New Orleans stores or say if they expect any changes in the local operation.

Since the beginning of the acquisition talks, local retail analysts have speculated that the new owner would close Marigny Brothers' Canal Street store, where sales have been sagging along with other downtown merchants, as retail trends have seen a shift to suburban shopping malls.

"I don't know of any plans to close this store," said Haywood Coleman, Store Manager at the Canal Street location, "but it would be a shame if it happened. This store is to New Orleans what Macy's is to New York City. It's not just a department store. It's a landmark, a gathering place for the whole community. And let's not forget, this store is the home of Mr. Bingle. What would Christmas in New Orleans be without him?"

Marigny Brothers, a leading chain in most of its markets in the Gulf South, has long been seen as a takeover target by retailers such as Federated Department Stores, May Department Stores, and Proffitt's.

"Marigny Brothers is the gem that everybody in the industry wants to acquire," Coleman said, "because we still believe in doing business the old-fashioned way – with a friendly smile, good value, and great service. In that respect we're a little behind the times, but that's what makes us special."

Chapter 1

"Smile, 'Wood, you're still the man in charge here," Haywood Coleman said to himself, stretching a tight grin across his face. "You've got to lead by example."

Even though his chest sagged under the weight of chronic worry, he played the part of the able manager. He strode past the Cosmetics Counter and checked himself in a mirror, straightening his blue blazer and red silk tie.

"Shouldn't have eaten that last piece of pecan pie," he grumbled, as he loosened his belt a notch. He couldn't complain, though. Approaching fifty, he still wore the same size pants as on his wedding day. He wrapped up the inspection by patting down his tight afro and leaning in close to the mirror to examine a wrinkle that had appeared under his eye.

"Hmm, so much for 'black don't crack,'" he muttered, recalling one of his mother's old sayings. An employee came into view, causing Coleman to stiffen.

"Merry Christmas, Miss Jackson," he said to

the young lady behind the counter who was tending to an oversized display of anti-wrinkle creams.

"Ain't Christmas yet," she said without the least hint of holiday cheer. "Barely Thanksgiving. Shoot, I couldn't even take the bus in tonight…because it wasn't running. Least the bus drivers got the night off. I don't suppose y'all gonna' be reimbursing my cab fare."

"Now come on, girl," Coleman said, forcing a smile. "That ain't no way to get this party started."

"Ha, don't look like no party to me," she said. Her volume trailed off, then picked up again. "You don't lock people in no party. Look like slave labor. Even Wal-Mart don't open till 6 a.m. Shoot."

"But we'll get us a head start," Coleman said. "Set us apart from the competition."

"No, it's our stingy paychecks set us apart," she said, "least since Mr. Fillmore come around."

Coleman didn't bother to argue because he knew she was right. He just shrugged and sighed.

Spinning around on his heel, he surveyed his staff's lethargic preparations, then checked his watch: 11:45 p.m.

Thanksgiving Night.

He could understand the lack of enthusiasm, given the circumstance. Coleman had grown accustomed to working nights, weekends, and all sorts of odd holidays. But this was a first.

Thanksgiving is supposed to be spent with family and friends. This year, under new ownership by Fillmore's, Coleman's store would be starting its "Black Friday Blowout Sale" at midnight, kicking off the holiday shopping season with a bang.

"Let's go, let's go," Coleman said, clapping his hands and shouting to no one in particular. "No frownin' or clownin'."

In the retail industry, "Black Friday" commonly refers to the day after Thanksgiving, supposedly when retailers go "into the black." To Coleman, it sounded like a bad horror flick.

Still, the dutiful foot soldier kept his chin up and a spring in his step. He had to motivate his team to reach new heights this year, especially with rumors swirling that the Canal Street store was on the company chopping block.

After 25 years at the same store, Coleman had certainly seen his share of change. At one time, Canal Street was *the* place to shop in New Orleans. Marigny Brothers, D.H. Holmes, and Godchaux's all had stores on the city's main street. Families would don their Sunday best and walk along the broad, flagstone sidewalk searching out bargains, maybe stopping into Woolworth's or Walgreen's for a treat at their now-extinct soda fountains.

He'd seen the city take out the streetcar to put in buses. He'd seen segregation, integration, and then white flight. With the opening of huge shopping malls in suburbs like Metairie and Kenner as well as across Lake Pontchartrain in Slidell and Covington, he'd seen a flight of another sort.

Business flight. Every year, it seemed, despite
working longer and harder, Coleman and his staff
struggled to keep pace.

Sure, the store was profitable. Coleman prided
himself on his tight fiscal management. But with
increasing competition, not only from the malls but
also from big-box chains and warehouse discount-
ers, Coleman fought a losing battle. Never mind the
store's place in New Orleans history. Never mind
the thousand little touches that made it special: the
rich, Italian marble floors; the hand-carved stone-
work; the elaborate window displays; the soft,
leather armchairs and plush, velvet sofas outside
the fitting rooms; the liberal cologne sampling
policy. It felt like your own private club, like you
were privileged just to gain admission.

And never mind the people: Frankie the pianist,
who could field any request with ease; Winston the
shoeshine man, who had the brightest smile on
Canal Street; Miss Doris in Women's Shoes (she'd
been there almost as long as Coleman), who knew
your size just by looking at you; and then there was
Pete the elevator man in the adjoining Marigny
Brothers office building. Who had an elevator man
anymore? Maybe that was the point.

Despite his best efforts, Coleman secretly
feared this Christmas might be his last on Canal
Street.

"Let's go, let's go," said a voice from the other
side of the shopping floor. It belonged to young

Willard Fillmore III, the braintrust behind this midnight madness, who barked commands from the Men's Department. "Clock is ticking. We need to pick up the pace."

Sent by his grandfather, Fillmore had been at the store less than two weeks and had already managed to alienate the entire staff, including his Store Manager.

"Merry Christmas, Mr. Fillmore," Coleman shouted as he approached. He addressed his District Manager in a formal tone, even though Fillmore was twenty years his junior.

Fillmore smiled politely. "Coleman, please, it's 'Happy Holidays' from now on. Got it?" Coleman nodded. "Page twelve in the manual. You have read it, haven't you?"

"Of course, of course."

Fillmore then addressed him the way a kindergarten teacher would a pupil. "Not all of our customers, or staff for that matter, are of the Christian faith."

"Right, right, got it," Coleman said, fighting the urge to roll his eyes. "Sorry about that."

Something in Fillmore's peripheral vision distracted his attention, and he directed his ire at Coleman. "Haywood, did you see what your people are doing to the cashmere?"

"My *people*, sir?" Coleman said.

"Yes," Fillmore said, swiping a hastily folded sweater from a tabletop display. He understood the implication of Coleman's reply but chose to disregard it. "*Your* people. Your staff. You did hire them, didn't you?" Without giving time for an answer, he continued. "Fabric of this quality must be presented in a way that accentuates its value." He refolded the sweater and placed it atop the pile, admiring his artful merchandising touch. "There, now have someone fix these right away."

"Yes, sir," Coleman said. "Soon as I have a free man. We're running short-staffed like you wanted."

"Good, good. And what about those budget estimates? Have you finished them yet?"

"About that, I've been meaning to talk to you."

"Yes, and?" Fillmore seemed agitated by this.

"And I wanted to ask one more time about the Christmas bonuses."

Fillmore threw out his hands. "Jiminy Christmas, man," he said, aggrieved by Coleman's persistence. "We're paying them time and a half for tonight. What more do they want?"

"We used to get double-time on holidays."

"*And* we're giving out honey-glazed hens."

"Hens?" Coleman said. "You mean you're giving out Christmas chickens? What happened to the hams?"

"They're Tysons. We got a deal."

Coleman glared. "So I guess that's a 'no' on the bonuses."

"You should be thankful you have a job at all. That's what I'd suggest."

"Hey, I'm not complaining," Coleman said. "I'm just thinking about the staff. There's gonna' be a lot of grumpy elves running around here when word gets out."

Fillmore stopped to address Coleman directly, as though he were about to offer sage wisdom. "Haywood, sometimes being the leader means having to make the unpopular decision."

"Guess you know all about that," Coleman said. Fillmore didn't know whether to take this as a compliment or an insult.

"It's in my blood," he said.

The men stood together, sharing an awkward silence. Just enough time for Coleman to size up his new boss, barely six months out of the MBA program at Southern Presbyterian University.

His soft, pink hands looked like they'd blister on contact with a broom. His thin, pointy nose and weak chin would probably shatter from the slightest of blows, not that Coleman had ever thought of punching him. He didn't believe in violence. But that's not to say the man-child standing before him couldn't use a good, old-fashioned butt-whoppin'. Once news of the Christmas bonuses spread, there would be a line of volunteers for the job.

MBA or not, Fillmore knew everything about price and nothing about value.

***

Minutes before opening, Fillmore called the staff together in the center of the store, at the base of the first floor escalator. Outside, the only prospective shoppers waiting were the vagrants huddled under the Canal Street overhang, trying to escape the light rain.

"What's this all about?" said a clerk from Housewares.

"Pep rally," replied a skeptical salesman from Electronics. This elicited a chorus of chuckles that rippled across the assembled throng.

"They say it's a new policy," said a stock clerk.

"Oh gimme' a break," said an older worker from the Fragrance Counter. "What kind of fools do they take us to be?"

A voice cut through the chatter.

"Quiet. Let's quiet down. Please. Quiet down now." It was Fillmore. As the staff gradually came into compliance, he cleared his throat and began to speak.

"I've tried to meet as many of you as I could. But in case I haven't, my name is Willard Fillmore the Third. You can call me Mr. Fillmore or, if you prefer, you can just call me 'Sir.'

"I'm the District Manager for Fillmore's Incorporated, overseeing all of our New Orleans stores. As you may know, my grandfather, Willard Fillmore the First, founded the company in 1952 in Waxahachie, Texas. Now that we have formally assumed ownership of Marigny Brothers, I will be doing everything I can to help Mr. Coleman, and all of you, make a smooth transition as we adopt Fillmore's corporate policies and practices.

"I want to thank each and every one of you for helping make this inaugural 'Black Friday Blow-out' sale a tremendous success. I know the shoppers of New Orleans will appreciate the extra time and extra savings, and I know that appreciation will be reflected in extra sales for Fillmore's."

"How about some extra money in our pay-checks?" someone in the crowd called out, creating a wave of laughter.

"Yeahyouright," shouted another employee.

"Come on, now," Coleman snapped. "Show some respect, and let the man talk."

"Thank you, Haywood," Fillmore said.

"Before we unlock the doors, I do want to take a moment to recognize someone special in our midst."

A murmur ran through the crowd.

"I happened to check our personnel records and discover that, on this very day twenty-five years ago, Haywood Coleman, your beloved Store Manager, joined the staff of Marigny Brothers as a stock boy."

With all the turmoil surrounding the takeover, Haywood had actually forgotten his anniversary with the company.

"Haywood Coleman represents everything that is good about Marigny Brothers, everything good about Fillmore's, and he serves as a shining example of what we all can achieve with hard work and dedication."

A genuine smile washed over Coleman's face, and he was truly touched by Fillmore's words.

"And so, Haywood, to commemorate twenty-five years of distinguished service – I know it was with Marigny Brothers, but, hey, we're all one big family now – I want to present you with this gold watch, one of the finest in our collection. May you enjoy another twenty-five more great years with Fillmore's."

He handed the watch to Coleman, and the two shook hands as the entire staff erupted in cheers. Coleman recognized the watch, recalling that it was a mere $24.95 wholesale. But it was the thought that counted.

This was most unexpected. Maybe Fillmore wasn't so bad after all.

"Now, enough of me. Would you like to say a few words, Haywood?"

Coleman stepped forward to speak and had to clear away the constriction in his throat. Could it be that he was fighting back tears?

'Wood, get a hold of yourself.

Coleman looked at the watch, then panned to take in his entire staff so his words might sink in.

"One day a long time ago, a poor little kid from the St. Thomas Housing Projects came to Marigny Brothers at Christmas because somebody named

Mr. Bingle was up on stage with Santa Claus, just giving away presents. The little kid never forgot that day. He didn't know anything about business, didn't know much about Mr. Bingle. But he knew this store must be magic.

"If they were giving away free Christmas presents to poor little children, then there was definitely something magic going on. And that little boy knew if there was magic going on, then this store was the place he wanted to be. So here I am."

"Yeahyouright," an employee shouted.

"You go, Dawg," shouted another.

"Sometimes," Coleman continued, "even after the long days and angry customers, sometimes, when you can put a smile on somebody's face, I'm telling you, it *is* magic. It is. And every one of us, every one, has that power inside. Thank you."

Coleman dropped his head and stepped back. The staff burst into applause again, this time even more thunderous than before. Cheers and huzzas rained down on him from all sides. Fillmore patted him on the shoulder.

"That was quite a speech," Fillmore said.

"It's all true," Coleman said.

"Heck, after that, *I'd* work for *you*."

"We might be able to arrange that," Coleman said, breaking into a smile, the earlier tension between the men evaporating.

"Okay, okay, let's wrap this up and head to your departments," Fillmore announced, shouting like a football coach. "I want to see smiles all around, and if there are any more questions, Mr. Coleman and I will be circulating on the floor."

The staff dispersed in a hundred directions. A team of window decorators raced past Fillmore carrying a large box laden with stuffed, white snow fairies of varying sizes.

"Whoa, whoa, whoa," Fillmore said, catching one of the men by the arm. "Where are you going with that?"

"We forgot to put out Mr. Bingle," said the older of the two decorators, a note of alarm in his voice. "We need to get these up right away."

"You forgot what?" said Coleman, who'd remained within earshot. "Come on, man, you got to get with the program." He reached into the box and pulled out one of the Mr. Bingle dolls.

The plush, white fairy wore an inverted ice-cream-cone for a hat, red-striped mittens, and he sported a pair of holly-leaf wings on his back. His cherry-red eyes and licorice smile instantly warmed Coleman's heart, recalling a simpler time. He felt an irrational urge to hug the doll like an old friend.

"I'm sorry, Mr. Coleman, we'll take care of it right away," the decorator said.

Fillmore raised his hand to quell the discussion. "Nonsense. You'll do no such thing."

"What you talkin' 'bout?" Coleman said.

"Didn't you get the memo?"

"What memo?"

"The Bingle memo."

"The Bingle memo?"

"The Bingle memo. It went out last week."

"Well, what did it say?"

"Here. You can read it for yourself. Fillmore reached into his pants pocket and produced a folded piece of paper, which he handed to Coleman.

Dear Fillmore's Manager:

We regretfully announce the retirement of a New Orleans Christmas icon, Mr. Bingle.

Effective this holiday season, all Fillmore's managers are to refrain from positioning Mr. Bingle dolls or likenesses on any store displays, advertisements, or external communications. All Mr. Bingle merchandise is to be collected and placed in the outgoing loading bay for proper removal and disposal.

In order to effect a seamless transition to Fillmore's corporate culture, a number of minor adjustments will be necessary. We appreciate your attention to this matter.

Sincerely,

Willard Fillmore I

"What's this all about?" Coleman said, shaking the paper. "Why didn't you tell me about this?"

"It came from the home office via email," Fillmore said. "That reminds me, you need to get in the habit of checking your email more often. So these kinds of miscommunications don't happen."

"Wait a second. My E-what?" Coleman said.

"Your E-mail. Electronic mail. It's the state-of-the-art communication system that we've just installed. From now on, we'll use email for all of our internal communications instead of that vile fax machine. It'll save us thousands. So rather than resisting, I'd suggest you acquaint yourself with the new system and get with the times."

"Don't put this on me. I'm a people person."

"I assure you, eliminating Mr. Bingle was an agonizing decision for my grandfather. He's a people person, too." Fillmore said this as though it were a character defect.

"And you couldn't have said something to me?"

"I didn't think it was appropriate for me to..."

"I'll tell you what's not appropriate: killing Mr. Bingle. That's what's not appropriate."

"We're not killing Mr. Bingle."

"Tell that to the children," Coleman said, his momentum causing him to sway toward Fillmore. "The children of New Orleans who love him. You can't do that to them. It'll break their poor hearts."

"Surely, Haywood, you're overreacting."

"I don't think so. His blood's on your hands."

"Oh come on now, man," Fillmore said, trying to defuse the situation with a laugh. "There will be plenty of Christmas...uh, holidays to go around. No one will miss him. Trust me."

"Ha." Coleman glared at Fillmore, unaware

that his right hand had tightened to make a fist. He handed the memo back. "That memo's all well and good, but what are you gonna' do about the store-front mannequin?"

"Excuse me?"

"That thirty-foot-tall mannequin they're gonna' be hanging with a crane tomorrow afternoon. Same as every Christmas for the last forty years. Far as I know, ain't nobody canceled that."

Fillmore rubbed his forehead, realizing the colossal oversight. "Oh jeez, I forgot about that."

"Hard to ignore a giant snow fairy with a big ice-cream-cone head hanging over the front door." A mocking smile crept across Coleman's face. "Guess you ain't gonna' kill Mr. Bingle after all."

Coleman and the two decorators began to laugh, further irritating Fillmore. But he refrained from answering as his mind searched for a solution. Meanwhile, Coleman reveled in his tiny victory. New Orleanians might never know how close they had come to losing their beloved Christmas mascot.

"Tell you what," Fillmore said. "I'm going back to my office to think about this. You keep an eye on things. Make sure we open at twelve on the nose."

"No problem," Coleman said. "It's under control." Without saying another word, Fillmore hopped on the escalator and disappeared, consumed by one thought: killing Mr. Bingle.

Chapter 2

The news trucks began arriving promptly at 10 a.m., lining up in the commercial parking zone along Canal Street. All the local news stations came – even an independent videographer hoping to cash in on the action.

The cameramen strapped on their equipment, while the reporters went over notes or refreshed their makeup. When Coleman learned of the commotion, panic set in. No doubt, the intrepid news gatherers had descended on his store for their annual stories about Christmas-shopping chaos. Problem was, business was slower than expected. Much slower.

"Look alive," Coleman said to Miss Jackson, who was sound asleep at the Cosmetics Counter, her head laid atop her hands, snoring lightly, a small trickle of drool oozing onto the glass.

Coleman rapped his wedding ring on the countertop, and the young woman jumped to attention, her eyes glazed with fatigue.

"Wake up, Miss J. We got visitors." Coleman

moved toward the Canal Street entrance and continued to mutter to himself. He drew a deep breath and prepared to greet his guests, assuming his role as affable host.

"Y'all a little late," Coleman said, attempting to address the entire horde. "We opened at midnight. Shoulda' seen the rush. They were lined up around the block. I think we're in a lull now...finally."

No one seemed to pay particular attention to the remark. "Is he here yet?" a cameraman barked.

Coleman's brow crinkled in confusion. "Here yet. Is who here yet?"

"Bingle," said a young female reporter. Coleman brought her into focus. She was the most beautiful Creole woman he had ever laid eyes on, next to his wife, of course. Her *Daily Doubloon* ID badge read "Hope Lawson."

"Bingle?" Coleman said. The news fortified his flagging spirits. He smiled and checked his watch. "Y'all a little early for that, aren't you? Usually do it around noon."

"Guy on the phone said 10 a.m.," Lawson said.

"Why y'all all of a sudden so excited 'bout us hanging him in front of the store? We do it every year. Y'all never filmed it before."

Another reporter chimed in, this one a stern looking man with hair frozen by an entire can of AquaNet. "He's never been flown in by a helicopter before."

"Say what!" Coleman said

"Tell me," Lawson said, shoving a tape recorder into his face, "what prompted Fillmore's to undertake such a dramatic entrance for Mr. Bingle this year? Is this just a publicity stunt to draw attention because of the store's declining sales? Is it true that Fillmore's is considering closing this store?"

Coleman threw up his hands, helpless. "I'm sorry, ma'am. You're asking the wrong person."

"But you are the Store Manager, aren't you?" Lawson said.

"Well, yes, but…"

"Maybe I can help explain." A voice came from behind Coleman: Fillmore.

"And you are?" Lawson said. The other reporters swarmed around, jabbing their mics toward anyone eliciting so much as a burp.

"Willard Fillmore the Third. District Manager of Fillmore's Incorporated. We've decided, rather on a whim, to whisk Mr. Bingle in by air, sort of as a symbol of our commitment to New Orleans." He rubbed his chin to give himself an intellectual air.

Coleman drew back his shoulders and lifted his head, puffing out his chest in pride. Guess his stance really had an impact on the young boy. He clapped Fillmore on the back.

"And you've cleared this all with the city and with the FAA," Lawson said, "given the amount of congestion on Canal Street, especially on a busy day like today?"

Fillmore tried not to wince noticeably. So many details. He brushed aside the question with casual aplomb. "Sure we have. It's all been taken care of."

Just then, the faint pop of helicopter rotors cut through the air. Fillmore, Coleman, and their guests cast eyes upward to find the source. In the distance, they saw not one but three tiny specks slowly approaching.

By this time, a vast crowd of onlookers had encircled the news crews, hoping for their shot on local TV. Two blocks down Canal Street, a pair of police cars flashed their lights and blared their sirens. At the intersection of Bourbon and Canal, one of the cars turned at a 90-degree angle to block traffic, while the second stopped directly in front of the store. The policeman remained in his car to issue an order via loudspeaker: "Clear the sidewalk immediately. Clear the sidewalk immediately."

Of course, the hubbub only attracted more attention and, soon, it seemed every single pedestrian on Canal Street was standing in front of Fillmore's.

The frustrated policeman jumped from his car and pushed his way through the mob, shouting, "I wanna' see the manager."

Alarmed, Fillmore prodded Coleman. "Haywood, you're a local. Why don't you go and talk to the man?"

Coleman cleared his throat and stepped forward. "Yes, sir, can I help you?"

"You the manager here?" the big, burly officer said, pointing to Fillmore's. A sheen of sweat glistened across his forehead, even though he'd walked but a few feet.

"Well, yes, yes, sir, I am. Haywood Coleman. Is there a problem, Officer…Duncan?" he said, reading the man's nametag.

Officer Duncan removed his hat and mopped his sweaty brow with his shirtsleeve. "For starters, you failed to file for a construction permit, and then there's the street closure and the threat to public safety." He sighed. "Then there's the FAA, and maybe even the FBI."

"FBI!" Coleman said. As the helicopters came into view, he spotted the lead chopper soaring down the center of Canal with the giant Bingle swinging underneath, suspended by two steel cables.

On the chopper's tail were a Bell 206B police helicopter and a U.S. Army Apache helicopter poised to blow Bingle out of the sky.

"Your pilot failed to file his flight-path with the Federal Aviation Administration," the officer said. "Far as we know, you're all terrorists and that's a bomb." He pointed to the giant, white paper maché snow fairy.

"Land your aircraft immediately," crackled the police helicopter's loudspeaker. The chopper carrying Bingle swung right then left. Bingle's right foot clipped a streetlight, giving off a cloud of white dust and sending a shower of glass onto the concrete below. Bingle emitted an ominous creak.

"Clear the sidewalk," Duncan screamed suddenly. "I want this sidewalk cleared."

Driving the wrong way up Canal, two more police cars screeched to a halt in front of the store, delivering a team of officers clad in riot gear. They began pushing onlookers away from the store entrance until a security perimeter was established at either end of the block.

The news teams fought in vain to maintain their freedom of mobility until, relenting, they jockeyed for position at the front of the pack.

Coleman, Fillmore, and Duncan remained at the store entrance, watching Mr. Bingle come into position. "You guys really porked the po-boy on this one," Duncan said. "But right now our number one concern is public safety. We'll discuss fines and jail time when this is over."

"Jail!" Coleman said. This time he was fully aware of his hand balling into a fist as he stared at Fillmore. "All taken care of, *my foot*."

Fillmore laughed his weasly little laugh and stepped toward Duncan. "Surely, this can all be worked out," he said, draping an arm around Duncan's shoulder. With reflexes belying his girth, Duncan spun Fillmore around and pinned the little punk's arm behind his back.

"You keep your hands right where I can see 'em, you got me boy? I ain't playing no more games with you."

Grimacing in discomfort, Fillmore tried to make amends. "I'm sorry, sir. Is there anything we can do at this point to make things right?"

The officer regained control of his temper and released Fillmore from his death grip. After wiping his brow one more time, he thought about it and chuckled, then motioned to the approaching mannequin.

"Yeah," he said, "get me one of them big Mr. Bingle dolls for my daughter. That's a start."

Coleman burst into laughter, hoping to deflate the tension. "I think we can do that. What do you think, Fillmore? You think we can find him a Mr. Bingle?"

"I'll tell you what I think," Fillmore started to say, but a voice from one of the helicopters overhead caught his attention.

"You have five seconds to bring the aircraft down," the police helicopter loudspeaker blared.

"What'll they do if he doesn't comply?" Coleman said. "You know it ain't no bomb."

"We can't take any chances," the officer said. "We're authorized to use force if we think there might be any danger."

"Aw, come on, there isn't any danger," Fillmore said. "It's Mr. Bingle, for crying out loud."

"You can't shoot him down in the middle of Canal Street," Coleman said. "Not with all these people standing around."

"We'll do whatever we gotta' do to protect the

people of Nooawlins," Duncan said.

"Oh, that's completely ridiculous," Fillmore snapped, causing Duncan to set upon him again.

"Listen, moron," Duncan said, poking Fillmore in the chest. "You're either with us, or you're against us. Now which is it?"

"FIVE...FOUR...," the police helicopter pilot announced from above.

Coleman screamed into the walkie-talkie that had been clipped to his belt. "Maintenance, this is Coleman, come in, come in."

"Yes, Mister Coleman, I'm here," a voice squawked from the radio.

"Is the installation crew in place? Get them up on the Canal Street overhang. Pronto!"

"Copy. They're all set."

Coleman stepped out into the street and watched a group of men climbing from a second-story window. They scurried about in preparation for the mannequin to be lowered.

"THREE."

Everyone turned their eyes upward, watching the helicopter struggle with its heavy load. The draft cast by the two pursuing aircraft hovering at its rear created an unusual wind current, causing Mr. Bingle to sway like a big, white pendulum. The creaking of the support cables reached an alarming pitch.

"They won't really shoot him down, will they?" Coleman said.

"Jeez, I sure hope not," Duncan said under his breath, noticing his police cruiser parked directly beneath Mr. Bingle.

"TWO."

Fillmore checked to see that the news cameras were rolling, catching all the action. He could barely contain his excitement.

"Just what kind of brain-dead pilot you got for this job, Fillmore?" Coleman said.

"Obviously a very good one," Fillmore said, watching the aircraft maneuver in front of the store. The remark struck Coleman as odd.

"ONE."

The crowd gasped in anticipation.

"WE HAVE NO CHOICE BUT TO BRING YOUR AIRCRAFT DOWN BY FORCE."

The helicopter carrying Bingle lurched at an awkward angle.

POP!

Rather than an explosion, it sounded like the twanging of a giant guitar string. The onlookers gasped again. Mr. Bingle hung in the air for a millisecond, fifty feet over Canal Street, then crashed to the earth like a rock. A direct hit on Officer Duncan's vehicle.

KAPOWWW!

The mannequin shattered into a million pieces and sprayed a cloud of chalky dust a hundred feet in every direction. Coleman, Fillmore, and Duncan cowered behind a sidewalk trashcan but were soon covered in white powder. Duncan took on the appearance of a mammoth sugar donut.

Fillmore let loose a gleeful yip and fought to suppress full-blown, joyous laughter, while Coleman and Duncan were near tears.

"Mr. Bingle!" Coleman said.

"My car!" Duncan said.

Looks of disbelief had washed over both of their faces. They turned to direct their anger toward Fillmore.

"Hey, look, fellas', this was all an accident."

In his peripheral vision, Coleman saw the unruly mob beginning to break free of the police line and, one by one, onlookers raced to the decomposing mannequin to collect souvenir hunks of paper maché.

"Hey, get back away from there," Duncan screamed, shaking his finger at the scofflaws. But the mob was too much for the law officers, who weren't particularly inclined toward violence, especially now that the threat to public safety had dissipated.

The three helicopters landed in a row in the middle of the wide street. As soon as the lead chopper touched ground, a law enforcement team that now included local police, sheriffs, FBI, and one agent from a top-secret bureau ripped open the cockpit door and threw the pilot to the ground, slapping cuffs on his wrists behind his back.

Duncan and his colleagues had lost all control

of the situation. Coleman feared that once the mob had picked Mr. Bingle's carcass clean, it would descend upon his store and commence looting.

"This is Coleman," he shouted into his walkie-talkie again. "Lock all doors. Control access at all entryways."

Amid the chaos and jostling from the restless crowd, Coleman felt a tugging at his sleeve. It was a short, Vietnamese man, carrying a long shoebox.

"I sorry, Mista Coleman," he said. "I try to get to work on time. But traffic real bad today."

It was Phan, the puppeteer, arriving to perform his Mr. Bingle marionette show on the store's special first-floor stage. Guess he didn't get Fillmore's memo either.

Fillmore stepped in, shook his head mournfully, and patted Phan on the shoulder to console him.

"Sorry, Phan, there won't be any show today." The puppeteer became extremely agitated. "But it not my fault. Police car block street so I couldn't get here on time."

Fillmore lifted his hand to calm him. "No, no, it's not that. It's Mr. Bingle."

"What wrong with Mista Bingle?" Phan said. He opened his box to reveal his Mr. Bingle puppet. "Mista Bingle fine. He right here."

Fillmore shook his head and pretended to be sad. "No, I think Mr. Bingle's dead." He pointed to the lifeless skeleton lying in the street, stripped of all dignity.

As quickly as it had materialized, the crowd dispersed once there was nothing left for the taking.

However, the news cameras continued to roll, capturing the overwhelming pathos of the scene.

"He dead?" Phan said in horror.

"I think so," Fillmore said, repeating it for emphasis. "Mr. Bingle's dead."

Chapter 3

When Coleman finally read the new manual
and figured out how to check his email, he found 17
messages in his In Box, all of which were memos
from Fillmore outlining new policies such as:

- the freeze on management salaries;
- the reduction of wages for new-hires;
- cuts in vacation and sick time;
- a new healthcare plan for full-timers,
  increasing the costs borne by employees;
- the new dress and appearance guidelines.

And then there was the Bingle memo.

Even though their offices were directly across
the corridor from one another, Coleman believed
Fillmore hid behind the cold, impenetrable shield of
email to convey these mandates, in part, because he
didn't have the courage to face the living, breathing
human beings the new policies affected.

Collectively, Fillmore's tactics for streamlining
the store would eviscerate its heart and soul. This,
in an effort to save it.

Despite a long list of problems that should have

occupied his thoughts – the small fortune in fines stemming from the helicopter fiasco; the lackluster "Black Friday" sales numbers; the cutting of the Christmas bonuses; even the embarrassment of handing out honey-glazed chickens – Coleman couldn't shake the traumatic image of Mr. Bingle's destruction from his mind.

He felt as though a part of himself were dying, and he refused to let it happen.

After the Bingle story broke, phone calls from anguished patrons had overloaded the voicemail system in Fillmore's Customer Service Department, where hours had been cut to keep costs down. Coleman had even taken a personal call from Cheryl LaBorde, president of the Mr. Bingle Fan Club and self-taught webmaster of mrbinglefriends.com. Coleman found the show of support encouraging, and he'd even gone so far as to promise LaBorde that (despite feeling otherwise) Bingle was safe.

Because Coleman still had one card to play: the daily Mr. Bingle TV show.

He bolted from his chair and sprinted across the hall to pitch an exciting new idea to Fillmore, who was typing furiously on his computer keyboard, no doubt hammering out yet another memo.

"I've got a great new idea for the TV spot," Coleman said, not even bothering to knock. He tried hard as he could to sound excited.

From Thanksgiving to Christmas Eve, Mr. Bingle's fifteen-minute puppet shows aired on

Channel 6 each weekday, just before the evening
newscast. In the early days of television, children
watched religiously, sitting mesmerized by the little
puppet. Although technically crude by modern
standards, the show had become a New Orleans
Christmas tradition and a part of the cultural
landscape alongside Mardi Gras, Jazz Fest, and
political scandal.

"We can have Mr. Bingle use merchandise from
the store as part of his show. You know, product
placement just like they do in the movies." Coleman
believed this appeal to Fillmore's baser instincts
would sway him. "What's better than a fifteen-
minute advertisement disguised as entertainment?"

Fillmore looked up, stopped typing, and smiled.
"It is a great idea, Haywood, but we're already
doing that. You should know that by now."

"Of course," Haywood said, "but I'm talking
about, you know, increasing the value of the
merchandise. You know, more expensive stuff."

"Exactly. We'll be implementing that very
strategy beginning with the season premiere on
Monday."

Coleman's face brightened. This kid was full of
pleasant surprises.

"Well allllright," Coleman said. "You know, I
was thinking, like, we could have Mr. Bingle ride in
on a toy train and talk all about trains, or we could
have him playing a new video game or, you know,
sporting some sharp little shoes, like some Baby

Jordans or…"

Fillmore cut him off before he got carried away.

"No, no, no, Haywood. I don't think you're following my meaning. We're going adult with this."

"Adult? But Mr. Bingle…"

"I'm with you, I'm with you all the way, Haywood. But Bingle won't be a part of it."

"What! What do you mean he won't be a part of it? I thought you just said..."

Fillmore shook his head, trying to convey some measure of compassion. "I'm sorry. The decision's been made. It's out of my hands. We're going to repurpose that program."

"Repurpose? What the heck does that mean?"

"Instead of some worthless puppet show, we're going to feature our hottest merchandise."

"But nobody's gonna' watch a fifteen-minute commercial. You've got to have a hook."

"Oh we'll have a hook alright." Fillmore slid a glossy photo across his desk for Coleman to examine. In it, a trio of scantily clad young women cavorted about a replica of Santa's workshop.

"Who's this?" Coleman said. "They look like B-girls working at Club Sho-Bar."

Fillmore found this amusing, and he chuckled. "*That*, my friend, is our hook."

"Look more like hookers."

Fillmore scowled. "They're Santa's special helpers. Santa's Playmates, if you will."

"I won't."

"Oh come on now. I thought this was New Orleans. *Laissez les bon temps roulez*."

"I thought this was a kids' show."

"Not any more."

Coleman threw the picture back at Fillmore. "This is a disgrace. An insult to the people of New Orleans, to Mr. Bingle, and to all of the people involved in building his legacy."

Fillmore sat back and began tapping his index finger on his desk. The wheels inside his brain began to rev.

"I admire the passion of your convictions." The compliment derailed Coleman's offensive, rendering him unable to respond. Fillmore leaned forward and rested both elbows on his desk. "So you really feel strongly about this, don't you?" He broke into a bemused grin, as though he found the sentiment precious.

"Yeahyouright," Coleman said.

Fillmore stood and poked his finger into the air. "Well maybe you *are* right."

"I *know* I'm right," Coleman said, indignant. He knew this kid had no spine. He'd be powerless to stand up to someone with real principles. Coleman sensed the tide turning once more.

Fillmore spread his hands wide to frame an imaginary camera shot. "What we need is a public farewell, a sendoff, a tribute to help soothe the public psyche. You know, like what they did for

Elvis, or Princess Di."

Coleman frowned. "They're both dead."

"Well, nothing that extreme. But a sendoff, nonetheless. As a way of saying, 'Thanks for the memories.'"

Coleman addressed Fillmore as he would an imbecile. "Junior, ain't you heard a word I said?"

"Of course I have. Trust me on this one."

"But you're still gonna' get rid of Mr. Bingle."

"I'm afraid I don't have any choice."

Coleman crossed his arms and rocked on his heels. "Mmm hmm." Just the night before, he'd experienced a vivid dream in which he'd flogged Fillmore senseless with a Hello Kitty umbrella.

"I've got an idea," Fillmore said.

"I've seen what come of your last idea. One more and they're gonna' shut us down for good."

"No, really, Haywood. We'll give Mr. Bingle the kind of farewell he deserves. He'll be a legend."

Coleman muttered a silent curse, wishing he could give Fillmore the kind of farewell he deserved.

***

The children of New Orleans didn't quite know what to make of it when the final Mr. Bingle show went live.

Instead of their favorite little fairy, they beheld a trio of leggy strumpets clad in candy-apple-red

Santa coats with white furry trim, knee-high black leather boots and cute, flouncy little Santa hats.

At least their character names were appropriate: Dancer, Prancer and Vixen.

Was this a lingerie pageant or a kids' show?

Coleman cringed as he stood behind the cameraman on the tiny set erected in the corner of his store, holding his breath in anticipation of how Fillmore's scheme would play out.

But then, down flew Bingle and up came the familiar song:

> *Jingle, jangle, jingle,*
> *Here comes Mister Bingle,*
> *With a message from Kris Kringle,*
> *Time to launch the Christmas Season,*
> *Fillmore's Stores make Christmas pleasin',*
> *Celebrate with gifts galore,*
> *Each a gem from…Fillmore's.*

Coleman still couldn't stomach those last two lines, having deviated from the original:

> *Gifts galore for you to see,*
> *Each a gem from…MB.*

The ladies sat astride an overstuffed, red armchair – Dancer and Prancer were sidesaddle on each arm, while Vixen, a pouty blonde, took the middle. Having plopped into Vixen's lap, Mr. Bingle appeared to be having the time of his life as the nymphs cooed over him and caressed his soft, white acrylic pile.

Vixen diverted her attention from Bingle and focused on a cue card next to the camera.

"Oh Mr. Bingle, I'm so sad that you have to go away to the North Pole to help Santa," she read, a slight pause as her eyes moved from line to line.

"Yeah," said Dancer, the redhead, who was stroking his little cheek. "We sure wish you didn't have to go."

In his squeaky, high-pitched voice Mr. Bingle tried to console his new friends.

"Don't be sad, girls," he said. "I'll always be right here." Bingle's little red-striped mitten tapped his heart.

"Awww, that's so sweet," the women said, unable to resist further stroking and petting and squeezing.

Coleman feared that, behind the set, Phan might get overly excited by the show of affection, considering that ventriloquists often suffer from psychological transference, internalizing the vicarious emotions of their dummies.

There was no such risk for Mr. Bingle's voice-man, Ray, a local drunk whom they'd hired a few years back after a dumpster-diving accident had rendered him a eunuch. Ray was one of the few males in the city who could match the trademark falsetto of Mr. Bingle's original voice-man and puppeteer, Oscar Eisenberg, who'd passed away after a long illness.

"You can't be sad at Christmas," Mr. Bingle said. "This is a happy time. Listen, I know how we can turn this into a magical celebration."

"How?" Prancer asked.

"We'll have a parade!" Mr. Bingle said.

"A parade?" Vixen said.

"You mean like Mardi Gras?" Dancer said.

"Exactly, only it'll be a Christmas parade."

"Oh, I just love Mardi Gras," Prancer said. Suddenly, as if she'd lost track of her surroundings, the dark-eyed brunette sprung from the chair and began to rip open her coat to expose the supple flesh underneath.

Coleman nearly burst onto the set to prevent a disaster on live television, but, fortunately, Prancer's flashback to her days at the Bourbon Cabaret quickly wore off, and she resumed her position on the chair.

Standing on the other side of the cameraman, Fillmore shuddered with glee. He slapped Coleman on the shoulder. "Haywood, are you seeing what I'm seeing? We've got ourselves an instant hit. This is brilliant. I'm talking genius. Absolute genius."

Coleman looked up just in time to see the parade "floats" assembling – a line of remote control cars and trucks – on which would ride a stuffed version of Mr. Bingle that had replaced the marionette. Along with him were stuffed versions of his sidekicks, Pete the Penguin, Bingle Bear, and Bingle Bunny.

From behind the set, Mr. Bingle's theme song began to play once again, and the floats started to roll. Secured to the front of each vehicle was a foot-tall, cylindrical object that was throwing off more sparks than a welder's torch.

"Those sure are some odd looking sparklers," Coleman said, watching balls of fire leap from the sticks and onto everything in their path.

"That's because they're not sparklers," Fillmore said. "They're roadside emergency flares."

"Come again."

"Flambeaux. Isn't that what you call them? To light his way. Like the old-line Mardi Gras parades. We want to be authentic, don't we?"

Coleman shrugged, trying not to worry about the smoke rising from the bowl of decorative pine cones on the coffee table next to the Christmas tree. It didn't seem to bother Santa's Playmates. They had risen to their feet and were bouncing up and down, waving at the procession of floats.

"Only the best for Mr. Bingle," Fillmore said. Coleman checked the ceiling to find the nearest sprinkler head. He returned his attention to the set just in time to see a glob of fiery goop come to rest upon Mr. Bingle's right foot.

"Uh, Fillmore?" Coleman said, pointing.

"What is it now, Haywood?"

"Remember those flame-retardant Mr. Bingle

dolls that I had put in the purchase order for?"

"Yes. Why?" Fillmore didn't hide his irritation.

"I'm assuming you never placed that order."

"Why are you bringing this up now?"

"'Cause it looks like Mr. Bingle ain't exactly flame-retardant. In fact, I'd say quite the opposite."

Tiny tongues of flame had now engulfed Mr. Bingle's lower extremities and were spreading upward. Compounding matters, a dozen other tiny blazes had ignited around the set, spreading among the wooden soldiers in the Nutcracker Suite and along the white furry trim of Vixen's coat.

"Well don't just stand there," Fillmore said. "Do something."

Coleman ran to the rear of the set, searching in vain for a fire extinguisher. On a table next to Ray was a large glass of water, which, obviously, he'd used to keep his voice hydrated during the show. Coleman snatched it up just as Ray was reaching for a swig.

"Heyyyy, you can't take that," Ray slurred.

"We got an emergency," Coleman said. He ran to the front of the set and took careful aim at Mr. Bingle, hoping to slow the advance of the flames just enough to finish the show. Coleman doused the doll with the water and held his breath.

POOF!

Fire engulfed the helpless doll almost the instant the liquid hit its mark. Flames leapt five feet into the air, and Mr. Bingle toppled from his perch, ironically, atop a remote-controlled fire truck. His red plastic eyes and cherry nose quickly melted into an amorphous hunk of charred, black goo.

Toxic smoke filled the cramped area, even filtering back behind the set and causing Ray to cough uncontrollably. Phan, on the other hand, was crying.

Santa's Playmates shrieked in horror and cast about for some means of helping. Prancer grabbed a cinnamon broom that had been hanging on the wall of the set, and she began beating Bingle's lifeless body until the flames died out and all that remained were scattered ashes and plastic chunks.

Coleman ran back to find an actual extinguisher, in the process discovering a bottle of Everclear – 180-proof, pure-grain alcohol – next to Ray's table. Phan still had not moved. He sat next to Ray, clutching his Mr. Bingle marionette, weeping over the horrific destruction.

Fillmore stood on the set, arms crossed, watching the escapade play out. It had gone even better than he'd anticipated. He held his hand over his mouth, trying to hide his wide smile.

Dancer, having discovered Vixen's coat ablaze, grabbed a second cinnamon broom from the wall and began beating her playmate with it.

"Owww, stop hitting me," Vixen said.

"But you're on fire," Dancer said.

Vixen looked down and saw smoke rising from her coat. "Oh my god, you're right." She also found a smoldering ember on Dancer's shoulder and shrieked. "Ahhh. You're on fire, too."

The two women began panicked hopping and, in seconds, had ripped off their coats, revealing holiday-themed lingerie, confirming Coleman's earlier suspicions.

The risqué turn of events pleased Fillmore immeasurably.

Just in time, Coleman returned to the set wielding a fire extinguisher and blasting everything in sight with its white, powdery mixture and obscuring the view of the television camera.

Not that it mattered. A minute earlier, the show's time had expired, and Channel 6 had already cut to its evening newscast, albeit with a breaking story:

MR. BINGLE DEAD
Fiery, on-camera accident claims life of New Orleans Christmas icon

This time Coleman knew it was true.
Mr. Bingle *was* dead.

Chapter 4

Edwin H. "Oscar" Eisenberg took a long pull from his scotch and peeked at the crowd from behind the curtain. It was the usual: drunks, perverts, hustlers, petty criminals, and mobsters.

Back in 1948, strip joints hadn't yet acquired the veneer of respectability that they would somehow enjoy in the years to come. They were pretty much rank dives frequented by the dregs of society, and Club Caligula at Bourbon & St. Louis was par for the course.

But as far as Oscar was concerned, it was the one place in town where he could ply his craft and earn a living wage, a truth he found not only ironic but also profoundly depressing.

He heaved a weary sigh, picked up his marionette, and prepared to take the stage.

"Ladies and gentlemen, just in from the Palace in Atlantic City," a disembodied announcer shouted over the PA system, "the hottest little lady in the land, the one, the only, Lana Lavalais."

The room went pitch dark except for the

spotlight trained on Lana. Dressed in black slacks and a black turtleneck sweater, Oscar blended into the background, allowing patrons to focus on Lana's flowing blonde mane and long, shapely legs. The music rose – a languid, floozy anthem – and Oscar propelled his puppet across the stage, tickling the strings to give her hips just the right amount of womanly swagger.

Only a master could make a puppet look sexy. With a dip and a wink, a twirl and a shake, Oscar had these fools hanging on Lana's every move. Even the working girls watched, hoping to pick up a few pointers.

Of course, Lana had several advantages over the humans. She didn't drink. Didn't demand tips. Didn't have a jealous boyfriend. And she didn't need hands to remove her clothes. Thanks to a few strategically placed strings, they disappeared from her body with a flick of Oscar's finger.

When Lana's star turn had concluded and a live human being had taken her place, Oscar returned backstage to his tiny room, removed his doll's blonde wig and clothes, and began its transition to Bubbles, the brazen brunette. A knock on the door distracted him. It was a worn, old stripper wearing pasties and a sequined g-string. She sagged in all the wrong places.

"Oscar, there's a man here to see ya," she said in a heavy New Orleans "Yat" accent.

Oscar looked up from his doll. "What?"

"Dis guy, he wants to tawk to ya."

Oscar groaned. Oh great, another pervert wanting a private dance from a puppet. Could it get any worse? He had to get out of this place. And quick.

"Ah, jeez, Frenchy, tell him I'm in da head." Even when delivering the gravest of statements, Oscar's squeaky voice took on a playful quality.

"But he ain't like dem otha' weirdos," she said. "Dis one looks normal. Says he wants to tawk bizness."

Oscar laughed. "Yeah, that's what they all say."

A young man stepped into the doorway. He wore a neat, gray flannel suit and held what looked like a shoebox under one arm.

"Excuse me, Mister Eisenberg, my name's Allen, Emile Allen." He extended his hand. Oscar just stared.

Why was this freak carrying around a shoebox?

"Well, I'll let the two of you alone to get to know one anotha' betta'," Frenchy said before scurrying off.

Allen pulled his hand back, intimidated. He broke into nervous laughter. "That's quite a show you got. You're very talented."

Oscar remained silent, barely acknowledging his visitor's presence as he lit a cigarette. He couldn't wait to hear what kind of bizarre proposition this one was going to come up with.

Allen scrambled to explain himself. "Mr. Eisenberg, I'm a window decorator at Marigny Brothers." He switched the box from one arm to the other, as though it had become too heavy to bear. "I'm a window decorator at Marigny Brothers, and I just got back from Chicago, where I went to Marshall Field's."

"Never heard of him," Oscar said.

"It's not a him," Allen said. "Well, I guess it is a him, or was. But now it's a store, a big store, and see, they have this Christmas character. Well, that's beside the point. The point is, it gave me this idea to create a Christmas character of my own. Well, not my own, New Orleans' own. A character that I want to put in our store so that when kids think of Christmas, they'll think of Marigny Brothers."

"The gambler?" Oscar said.

"No, Marigny Brothers," Allen said. "Oh, I get it. Marigny *was* a gambler. But I want them to think of the store when they see my character."

Oscar nodded, growing impatient. "Yes, and?"

Allen fumbled with his shoebox and removed a furry white snowman with a pointy hat and red-ribbon bowtie. "And so I came up with this little guy. Meet Mister Bingle. He's a snow fairy. Santa's special helper. My boss actually came up with the name. Got it from an old book. Get it? Mister Bingle. MB? Same initials as…"

"Yeah, I get it, I get it. Very clever. So what the hell's your snow bunny…"

"Snow fairy."

"Snow fairy, yeah, whatever. What's he got to do with me? I'm a puppeteer."

Allen dropped the box so that he could hold Mr. Bingle by both arms. "Well, my boss wants me to build a set in our Canal Street store and have somebody put on a puppet show every day throughout the Christmas season." He began to wiggle Bingle's arms. "My boss thinks that'll bring kids into the store. And when the kids come into the store, so will their parents, who'll buy stuff."

Oscar's eyes opened wide, and he bolted upright. He mashed out his cigarette and took the Bingle doll in his arms. Slowly, a smile crept across his face as the realization set in.

"And your boss wants me to…?"

"If you would consider it," Allen said. "He says you're the best. So he's been told."

Oscar looked up from the doll. The best? He drew his shoulders back proudly. "Well, of course I am. There's none better."

"Then you'll consider it?"

Oscar contemplated his grim surroundings. "Well I *am* quite happy here. I'm not inclined to leave on a whim."

"We'll give you complete artistic freedom, uh, sort of," Allen said. "And you'll do three shows an hour, six days a week."

Oscar rubbed his chin, feigning hesitation. "But you're talking about seasonal work. I don't know if

I can afford to quit here and…"

"Whatever they're paying you here, I've been authorized to double it. Whatever it takes."

This last offer hit home. Oscar smiled. "Whatever it takes, huh?" He could see Allen was uneasy with the negotiation.

"Well, within reason."

"What about the kids?"

"Kids? There'll be plenty of kids at the store."

"Not at the store. What about the ones who can't make it to the store? What about the poor kids? Or the kids in the hospital? I think Mr. Bingle should go to them. Put on a show. Put a smile on their faces. Make Christmas magic for them. What do you think?"

"I think my boss…"

"I didn't ask what your boss thinks. I asked what you think. You can think for yourself, can't you?"

Though caught off guard by Oscar's gruff manner, Allen was relieved and pleasantly surprised by the virtuous proposal. "I think that's a brilliant idea, sir."

"Don't call me 'sir.' Call me Oscar."

"You got it, Oscar. Then we have a deal?"

"It's a deal." The two men shook hands.

A tear formed in the corner of Oscar's eye. He offered silent thanks to whichever deity had seen fit to bestow this tiny miracle upon him, and then he slapped Allen on the back.

Frenchy stepped into the doorway, startled by the display of affection between the two men. "Oh, glad to see y'all gettin' along. Oscar, ya back on in two minutes."

Allen collected his box. "Well, I'll let you get back to work." He picked up the Bingle doll and handed it to Oscar. "I'll leave this little guy here so you can get to know one another."

"I'll get him strung up and ready to go," Oscar said. He set Mr. Bingle on his chair and prepared to take the stage with Bubbles the brunette. It was the happiest he'd felt in years.

"Oh, and one last thing," Allen said.

"What's that?"

"Merry Christmas."

"Merry Christmas to you, Emile. Merry Christmas." Oscar smiled. Such a nice sentiment. *Merry Christmas.*

As he watched the young man walk out of Club Caligula, Oscar didn't have the heart to tell his new friend that he was a Jew.

***

Coleman woke with a start, sensing someone was standing over him. When he opened his eyes, he beheld his wife Berniece, arms akimbo, wearing her green satin robe and a frown.

"Holding on ain't gonna' bring him back, 'Wood," she said, shaking her head and leaning down to remove a stuffed animal from his grasp. "You're gonna' have to let go."

Before he could get his wits about him, she had pried the creature free and taken it hostage. Coleman brought Berniece into focus and then the object under her arm.

"Mr. Bingle?" he said in surprise.

Where did that come from?

He sat up and examined his hands like they had operated independently of his control.

"No, baby. Reginald," Berniece said. "You must've been sleepwalking again."

"But I don't remember…"

"Course you ain't gonna' remember," Berniece said. "That's why they call it sleepwalking. 'Cause you were asleep." She sat down on the edge of the bed and placed a comforting hand on his lower leg. "You need to stay out of Reginald's room. That's only gonna' make it harder."

Coleman was still grappling with the mystery of the stuffed Bingle doll. Maybe she was right. Maybe he had been sleepwalking. No doubt Bingle had been on his mind constantly over the past week. With Mr. Bingle wrapped so tightly around the memory of his son, watching the doll's spectacular demise was almost like watching Reginald die all over again. And it brought back to the surface feelings it had taken him years to bury. Coleman shook his head. "I'm sorry, baby. I don't know."

"I know, I know," Berniece said, patting his leg.

The mattress sagged under her weight. She'd probably put on fifty pounds since the day of the funeral. "Maybe it's time to clean out the room."

Coleman's eyes bulged, and he felt like she'd driven a dagger through his heart. He choked on his own saliva and began coughing. "What? We can't do that. Not yet!"

"Baby, you get like this every Christmas, for the past five years," she said, resting her forehead in her hand. She'd grown so weary of this conversation. It played like an old movie, always with the same frustrating ending. "It's time to move on."

Coleman reached out and picked up the doll. "Guess I ain't ready yet."

"You ain't never gonna' be ready, 'Wood," she said. "You're just gonna' have to do it."

He sighed and stared at the doll. "Feels like everything's falling down around me. At the store. Fillmore. Reginald. Now Bingle. Feels like I need to hold on to something, to keep from slipping myself."

"We got each other, baby," Berniece said. "Ain't that enough?"

Coleman lifted his head to look at her, but his eyes focused on a point a thousand miles away. His heart was sinking into a bottomless pit, and he was powerless to pull himself out. Berniece mistook his paralyzing fear for a negative response, and she immediately threw up a protective wall.

"I ain't gonna' take this no more," she said,

bouncing from the bed and heading for the shower. "I can't help you if you can't help yourself." As she called out from the shower, her words echoed inside Coleman's head. "Reginald may be gone, but we ain't dead yet."

Jolted to action, Coleman hopped from the bed and threw on some clothes, resolved to remain among the living.

Two hours later, he found himself back at Willard's carrying news of an offer so incredible, Fillmore wouldn't be able to pass it up. Having called an old Dillard University classmate who now worked as Production Manager at Heart & Sons Mardi Gras World Headquarters, Coleman had negotiated a deal to reconstruct the giant storefront Mr. Bingle likeness for nothing more than the cost of the materials. Since float builders specialized in crafting oversized paper maché figures, Coleman had a hunch they'd be equipped to handle the job.

Furthermore, Coleman's buddy, Marcus Butler, would push the project through so that Bingle could be ready for mounting in front of Marigny Brothers a full week before Christmas.

Coleman raced to the store to give Fillmore the news and found him, as usual, in his office. But rather than typing another memo, he was examining a strange-looking doll.

"Haywood," Fillmore said, startled by his unexpected visitor standing in the doorway. He yanked the doll off his desk and dropped it beside his chair. "What are you doing here on your day off? You should be at home getting some rest."

Coleman wanted to tell him about his plan, but something in the little weasel's demeanor upset his progress. Fear. That's it. He saw fear.

"What's that?" Coleman said, pointing to the object on the floor.

"What? Oh that?" Fillmore said, shooing away the doll. "It's nothing. Just a prototype."

"Prototype? Prototype for what?" Coleman walked around the desk and attempted to reach for the doll, but Fillmore blocked his path.

"Damn, boy, why you buggin'?" Coleman said. "Just lemme' see the thing."

Fillmore reluctantly handed over the doll for Coleman to inspect. If Ernie & Bert had conceived a love child with Smurfette, this creature would be the unfortunate result. Bluish skin, bug eyes, gap-toothed smile and a wiry shock of white hair atop an asymmetrical head.

Coleman recoiled at the sight. "Thing looks like Chucky," he said, referring to the villain from the B-movie cult-classic "Child's Play," a red-haired doll possessed by Satan. Fillmore scowled and motioned for the doll so he could take another look.

"He does not look like Chucky. His name is Johnny Winter."

"Well what's wrong with his eyes? He looks possessed. Or something."

Fillmore did have to admit, the doll's cross-eyed

stare was a bit unsettling. "Um, there was a little
mix-up at the factory. My instructions were lost in
translation, I guess. Damn Chinese."

Coleman glanced down at Fillmore's desk,
spotting what appeared to be a proof for a new ad
in the *Daily Doubloon*. Even upside down, he
could make out the words, "Introducing Johnny
Winter, Fillmore's wonderful Christmas elf."

Coleman felt the anger rising in his chest, but
he couldn't tell if it was directed toward Fillmore or
at himself for having been such a fool.

Fillmore took the opportunity to defend his
actions. "Haywood, I know what this must look
like, but you have to know a lot of careful planning
went into this decision. We've done customer
surveys, focus group testing. Johnny Winter
appeals to the broadest demographic cross-section
of any doll we've ever tested."

"But that thing looks like Chucky. Ain't nobody
gonna' buy no presents from a doll look like
Chucky. Don't need a focus group to tell you that."

Fillmore remained patient. This was business,
he reminded himself. "Please, Haywood, if you
could just put your emotions aside…"

"This ain't emotion. This is common sense."

"Our research showed that Mr. Bingle was too
closely identified with Marigny Brothers, and to
shift the store's image in the market, we
needed…"

"To kill Mr. Bingle."

"Not kill him. Don't be ridiculous."

"Well what do you call what happened? You dropped him a hundred feet from a helicopter."

"That was an accident."

"You burned him to a crisp on live TV."

"An accident, too."

"And you got your little Santa's hos dancing around the puppet stage like strippers."

"Also an…I beg your pardon, they are not 'hos,' as you so rudely suggest. They're Santa's Playmates."

"I know hos when I see 'em. They're hos."

"Haywood!"

"Now you got this cross-eyed Chucky Winter."

"It's Johnny Winter."

"It's wrong is what it is. Congratulations, Fillmore, you got your Christmas wish. You finally did it. Mr. Bingle's gone. He's dead."

"Oh give me a break."

"You kill Mr. Bingle to celebrate Jesus' birthday. That's original. Merry Christmas. Ho ho ho. Merry Christmas. Joy to the world, the Lord is come…"

Coleman turned and left the room, tossing his plan for Mr. Bingle's salvation in the trash can on the way out.

Fillmore let loose an agonized groan. He didn't have the heart to tell Coleman he was an Atheist.

And that Coleman was fired.

Better to dash off a quick memo.

Chapter 5

Willard Fillmore I sat on the floor in his spacious Dallas office surrounded by toys. Though he'd never admit it to anyone, this was his favorite part of the job. He liked to call it quality control. But to the objective observer, it looked like a silly old man playing with toys.

Wielding a remote control, Willard navigated a jacked-up four-by-four over a mountain of stuffed animals. Then, his attention waning, he set down the remote and grabbed an updated version of the classic ViewMaster loaded with a slide show titled "Dinosaurs in 3-D." Holding it up to his eyes, he tilted his head toward the bright light streaming in from the twenty-second-story windows.

His office door swung open, and in walked an officious-looking fifty-something woman.

"Mr. Willard, your grandson's on the line."

Willard continued to stare into the ViewMaster, oblivious to the woman's presence. He elicited a muffled roar, as though giving voice to the mythical creatures before his eyes.

"Mr. Willard," she said. He dropped the toy and frowned like a child who'd been called in for dinner, even though he really did want to take the call.

"Thank you, Donna," he said. "It's about time that little scamp called me back," Willard said. He struggled to get to his feet, holding out his arms so that Donna could give him a hand. Despite heading a multi-million-dollar company, Willard played up the notion that he was, at heart, still just a big kid.

"Heyyy, Big Willie," Willard said, picking up the phone at his desk and sitting in his plush, leather office chair. He spun around and kicked his feet up onto the plate glass of the floor-to-ceiling window, the phone cord wrapping around him. "Don't you ever return your messages?"

"Grandpa, please," Fillmore said, impatient. "No more with the 'Big Willie.'"

"Ohhh, I'm just teasing," Willard said, chuckling. "Whatever happened to my little buddy?"

"He grew up and went to work."

Willard almost seemed hurt. "That doesn't mean you have to lose your sense of humor. This is supposed to be fun."

"I'm young enough as it is," Fillmore said, on the defensive. "I don't need to give *these people* any more reason to disrespect me. They seem to have plenty enough as it is."

All the way from the company headquarters, Willard could smell trouble brewing in New Orleans. Forty years in this business taught him that in order to get respect you had to give it. In two simple words, the boy showed he did not yet grasp this tenet of sound management, MBA notwithstanding.

Willard wanted to give his grandson a fair go, let him learn on the job. But something in his gut didn't sit right. Something more than the recent barrage of complaints. He knew there would be hiccups during the takeover, always were. He knew people would leave, egos would be bruised, criticisms made. He was used to all that. But this was different.

It was something in the boy himself, a certain cold detachment, a latent hostility. Too much shuffling from one parent to the other in the boy's youth. Too many violent video games. Too little time with his father, Willard II, who'd abandoned his family in order to cruise the Caribbean in his beloved, 36-foot catamaran. Plain and simple, the boy needed love. But deep down, Willard feared he'd placed a cyberpunk in a role requiring a people person.

"I'm sorry I didn't call you back sooner, Grandpa," Fillmore said. "I've been out on the floor. Didn't you get my emails?"

"Ha!" This suggestion struck Willard as humorous. "Emails? It takes me fifteen minutes just to type my cotton-pickin' name. I don't have time for email."

"It's meant to save time, Grandpa. That's the

idea. It's the future of business communication."

"I want to save time, I pick up the phone, not play some computer game," Willard said.

"It's not a game. It's..." Fillmore sighed on the other end of the line. This debate was going nowhere. "Well, at the very least, you should have Donna check your email."

"Thankfully, she read your mind and brought me your latest memo. I'm trying not to get worried over here, but you're making it difficult."

"Oh come on, Grandpa, don't worry. Hey, did I tell you about my honey-glazed hens idea?"

"You mean the Christmas chickens? You're really going to go through with that?"

"We'll save five thousand dollars."

Willard rolled his eyes. "Well, maybe, but that's not the point. It's the thought that counts."

"But I thought you said we need to tighten..."

"Fair enough. I guess it's a judgment call. It's knowing what to cut and what to leave."

"So are you saying you want me to reinstate the Christmas bonuses?"

"You cut the Christmas bonuses!"

"But I thought...giving away money..."

Willard set down the phone and rubbed his forehead. Maybe this boy was too green for the task. He obviously needed more guidance than he'd originally thought. "Now I hope you've been working closely with Haywood on this. What does he think about it?"

Fillmore gulped. "Ahh, I don't know about Haywood. He's kind of old-school, you know."

"Yes, I do know. I'm kind of, as you say, old-school. Our business is kind of old-school. What's wrong with that?"

"It's just, he's one of those 'that's not how we used to do it' kind of people. He's so negative."

"You cut my bonus and give me a Christmas chicken, I'd be negative too."

"He's become an impediment to progress, more like an enemy than an ally."

Now it was Willard's turn to sigh. "Look, Big Willie, uh, son, Haywood Coleman is the longest-tenured employee on the staff. Think of him as a resource, not an adversary. And there's something else you need to understand. He's an important symbol for the company, because he's a link with the Marigny Brothers tradition. If we forget that, we'll alienate the people of New Orleans. And if we alienate the people of New Orleans, we won't have a business in New Orleans. Understand?"

Willard heard silence on the line. "Which reminds me. I'm sitting here looking over the November expenses, including that ten-thousand-dollar fine from the City of New Orleans. Has the Mr. Bingle situation been taken care of?"

"Oh yeah, it's fine. Everything's under control. No problems here. Bingle's been fixed."

"That was quite a stunt you tried to pull," Willard said, as a smile washed over his face.

"Sounds like something I would have done back in my younger days. Chalk that one up to youthful exuberance. I hope you've learned your lesson."

"Yes, Grandpa, I have. It won't happen again."

"Good, now what's this I hear about a problem with the TV spot?"

"Oh, just some creative differences with the staff. I brought in some new talent. You know how artsy types can get. Nothing to worry about."

Willard shuffled another paper across his desk. "And who is this Johnny Winter? I thought he was a guitar player. You know, that albino guy?"

"Oh him, uh, that's nothing."

"Nothing? I've got a bill here for five thousand dollars worth of 'nothing.'"

"Well, I've been meaning to talk to you about this. You see, with the money we saved on the Christmas chickens, I thought the store could use a new Christmas mascot, something to separate Fillmore's image from Marigny Brothers, something distinctly ours. So Johnny Winter is the prototype. But it's still a work in progress."

"I say, that's a great idea. You can have this Winter fellow and Mr. Bingle work hand-in-hand. You know, create a bridge from the old to the new."

Willard felt encouraged for the first time in the conversation. Maybe he'd misjudged his grandson. Maybe he needed to give him space. Sure, he'd make a few mistakes. But nothing that couldn't be fixed.

"Johnny Winter, huh?" Willard said.

"That's our guy."

"I like it. Johnny Winter and Mister Bingle. I want you to work with Haywood on it. And cut him a little more slack. You could learn a lot from him."

"Uh huh."

Willard set his feet back on the floor and spotted a toy that had yet to be tested. "Well, I've got to get back to work. Try to stay in touch. Keep me posted here. Your old grandpa gets worried."

"Okay, Grandpa, I will. I promise. Love you."

"I love you, too. Bye now." Willard scampered over to unwrap the new *Godzilla* action figure set, sensing he'd set the boy straight.

***

Fillmore hung up the phone and drifted into a daydream, in which he explained to his grandfather how things really were. He almost felt pity for the old man, so out of touch with the modern work-place. The new breed of corporate warrior was a mercenary, loyalty a thing of the past. Forget what those New Age types said. It was all about the bottom line. Survival of the fittest. Kill or be killed.

Fillmore secretly feared the store was losing its edge in the marketplace. To his way of thinking, the problem stemmed directly from leadership at the top. Something had to be done, and he was the one to do it. Who better to replace his grandfather?

But first things first. If Haywood Coleman had to be the sacrificial lamb in order to move the company forward, then so be it.

In the midst of his fictional discourse on management philosophy, Fillmore heard the office door across the hall open. He rose from his desk and found Coleman putting on his company blazer.

"What are you doing here?" Fillmore said, his heart pounding in his chest. Why was he so nervous all of a sudden? Perhaps the gods were testing him. Yes, exactly. This was a test.

"You said that last time. I work here."

Fillmore shook his head and leaned against the door frame for support. "I take it you didn't get the memo."

"What memo? Ain't we had enough memos!"

"The email. We've discussed the need to regularly check your email. It's very important."

"How important can it be that you can't say it yourself?" Coleman tugged at his cuffs and adjusted the blazer, only pretending to care. "I'm here now. Tell me. What did that memo say?"

"It said, 'You're fired.'"

Fillmore had his full attention now.

"Say what!"

"I'm sorry, Haywood. There's no other way. Our management styles conflict, and it's created an insurmountable problem."

"Wouldn't be no problem if you'd act like a human being instead of a business school robot."

"I am a human being," Fillmore said in a stilted, mechanical voice. It sounded like he was trying to convince himself and not doing a very good job of it. "I have feelings."

"Funny, you don't act like it."

"Look, this is business. It's nothing personal."

Coleman laughed. "Oh, it's personal alright." He leaned in on Fillmore, poking him in the chest with each accusation. "When you cut salary, when you take away people's health insurance, when you make 'em work Thanksgiving night, when you kill their lil' Christmas dolls in front their very eyes, there's lives you're affecting, people you're hurting. That don't bother you?"

Fillmore was now backed up against the wall, and he actually feared for his physical safety, having recognized the look in Coleman's eyes. It was the same look that Mike Tyson got just before pulverizing an opponent in the ring or biting off a hunk of his ear. The look terrified him, but he was paralyzed. Nothing in his course work dealt with confronting an irate employee on the verge of violence.

Fillmore scanned the deep recesses of his brain and, having no real-world experience to draw from, produced a hackneyed, textbook platitude. "Uh, uh, Haywood, uh, as a manager, I, uh, sometimes I have to sacrifice the, uh, the well-being of a few for the good of the many."

Coleman backed off slightly.

"Ha! Show me the many. I don't see 'em. All I see is a bunch of grumpy wage-slaves."

Fillmore regained his equilibrium and launched a desperate broadside of his own.

"The many, in case you fail to recognize them, are all those men and women out on the floor who still have jobs," he said, waving his hand. "They'd be unemployed if you had your way, because this store would be closed."

An alarm sounded in Coleman's head. Something didn't add up. He recalled a conversation he'd had with the boy's grandfather when the acquisition talks first began. Seemed like a nice old man. Coleman knew people, and he trusted him. This was all out of character for Willard Fillmore I, but maybe not for Fillmore III. The recent events had the boy's fingerprints all over them. Coleman drew a breath and cocked his eye.

"Does your grandfather know about this?"

Fillmore swallowed hard. "Of course he does. He's, he's the one who authorized me to do this." A taunting smile crept across Coleman's face.

"Maybe I need to call him. Just to make sure we're all on the same page."

Fillmore motioned to the phone on the desk. "Go ahead. Be my guest. I'm afraid it won't change anything."

Coleman stared at the phone.

"The old man'll only confirm what I've already told you."

Coleman reached for the receiver and poised his hand to dial. Fillmore tried to appear cocksure, but inside, he fumbled for a way to prevent the call.

"I'm serious. Go ahead," Fillmore said.

Coleman realized he didn't know the number to the corporate headquarters.

Fillmore made one last attempt to solve the problem. When in doubt, throw money at it.

"I can tell you that my grandfather's authorized me to give you a generous severance package," Fillmore said. "And a good reference should you seek other employment. If you go stirring up trouble, I won't be able to guarantee anything."

Coleman slowly set down the phone and gave a cynical laugh. "Maybe I'll go down the street to Macy's. Bring Bingle with me."

"Do what you must, but I'm afraid Bingle stays. When we bought all of Marigny Brothers' assets, we bought the trademark for the doll as well. He's not going anywhere, except to the incinerator."

Coleman's spirit sank even though he vowed to press on with the fight. His mind raced to find new points of attack. But ultimately rendered impotent, he was forced to acknowledge defeat.

Fillmore breathed deep in his victory and fancied himself the magnanimous, conquering hero. In the end, he came off haughty and condescending.

"Well, then, Haywood, I'd like you to collect your things as quickly and as quietly as possible so that we don't have an ugly scene."

"I've been here twenty-five years. I think I'll take as long as I damn well please."

Fillmore shook his head and laughed, admiring his adversary's stubbornness. "Look, you can do this quick and quiet, or I can have the security guards escort you out. Your choice."

Coleman removed his jacket and began to roll up his sleeves in preparation for the task of clearing out his office. His eyes burned with loathing.

"Don't worry. I've got too much pride to make a jackass of myself."

***

Coleman moved through his office in a daze, throttled by the realization that his life's work had come to this ignoble conclusion.

It didn't take long to gather his belongings, because he didn't have many in this cold, cramped box. Most of his time had been spent out on the floor with his staff and customers, and the truly valuable things he'd acquired during his tenure were the thousands of friendships he'd made. Fortunately, he'd be taking those with him.

Maybe it was best to leave quietly, as Fillmore had suggested. He wasn't much in the mood for socializing, hated goodbyes, and he wasn't sure he could stomach any kind of big sendoff. Not that anyone would have time for one. Christmas was rapidly approaching, and the pace on the sales floor had picked up considerably.

Before leaving, Coleman made one final trip to the warehouse, where the refuse of Mr. Bingle's life had been heaped into a dozen battered boxes and set out for disposal.

You and me both.

The cavernous space was as cold and quiet as a tomb. Coleman spotted his quarry in the far corner, just off the loading dock. To access it, he had to climb over damaged furniture, broken kitchen appliances, and faulty sporting goods equipment, all awaiting return to their manufacturers. Upon reaching the first box, he ripped off the packing tape and pried it open to find a vintage, three-foot-tall Mr. Bingle lamp, made of glass, that used to serve as a backdrop in Santa's Workshop. He lifted it out of the box and set it on the cement floor.

They can't throw this away! It's priceless.

He moved to the next box and found a collection of Styrofoam Bingles, which had once hung from the store's ceiling, suspended by invisible wire. He remembered the way children would marvel as the air currents spun them around.

Oh, man, this ain't right. Got to do something.

He searched desperately for a solution. He was running out of time and options. He started toward another box but was distracted by a noise coming from across the warehouse. He looked up to investigate.

It seemed to be emanating from a pile of defective electronics, and it was growing louder. He walked toward the source of the noise and saw a bluish light coming from a television. The sound was faintly recognizable though garbled.

As he drew closer, he saw that the set was on. Odd, perhaps, but he recalled the many times he'd caught employees having a cigarette break and watching a football game on one of the damaged TVs. Nothing unusual there. He reached down to turn off the set and froze at the sight.

The music came into focus, as did the picture. On the screen, in grainy black & white, was Mr. Bingle, accompanied by his theme song, performing on his daily television show. By the look of it, the show must have been circa 1960, maybe earlier.

Coleman dropped to his knees and placed his hands on the set's chipped walnut cabinet. He saw a line of children streaming past the puppet, while a human attendant handed out presents. At the rear of the line, he saw a wiry, black boy, dressed in a neat white shirt and bow-tie, patiently awaiting his turn. Coleman touched the screen where the image of the boy moved. His bottom lip began to quiver.

A light flickered over near the Bingle boxes. He looked up and saw the Bingle lamp, glowing brightly. Floating in the air above it were a trio of the Styrofoam dolls. He stood and stumbled toward the apparition but stopped when he felt a tugging at his leg. He looked down. It was a stuffed Mr.

Bingle doll at his feet.

"AHHHHH."

Reacting from instinct, Coleman punted the doll across the warehouse. It hit a discarded computer terminal, which came to life with an audible beep. Having lost his composure, Coleman ran to retrieve the doll and began apologizing profusely. He picked the doll up from the keyboard and beheld a single word on the blank screen: "HELP."

Even the computer gods are mocking me!

Coleman blinked hard, only to find every electronic device blaring Mr. Bingle's theme song throughout the warehouse.

He picked up the doll and ran back to Fillmore's office, hoping the apparition would inspire in his nemesis a magical change of heart.

"What is it now, Haywood?" Fillmore said. "I have to warn you, I've already put security on notice should you try anything funny."

"No, no, you've got to come see this," Coleman said, breathless.

"Come see what?"

"Bingle. He's…it's…come see." Coleman grabbed Fillmore's shirt and pulled him into the hallway with alarming force.

"Get your hands off of me, you crazy bastard."

Coleman had a look in his eyes that was even more unsettling than before.

"Come on." He tried to grab Fillmore again by the arm. Fillmore pulled a walkie-talkie from his belt clip and shouted into it.

"Security. To my office. Code red. Code red."

"No, Fillmore, look." Inch by inch, Coleman dragged him down the hallway. If only Fillmore could see for himself, he would believe.

In seconds, two burly security guards had raced to the second floor and set upon Coleman, who began shouting and flailing. Gripping the Bingle doll, he proceeded to beat one of the guards over the head to no avail.

"Nooo, Fillmore, you can't…"

"Oh thank God you made it here when you did," Fillmore said to the guards, straightening his shirt and tie. "He was going to kill me."

"Nooo, I just want to show you…"

Coleman still wrestled with his captors, but it was clear he no longer posed a threat to Fillmore, who resumed a calm, professional demeanor.

"I'm sorry, Haywood, I gave you a choice." Fillmore turned to the guards. "Get him out of here. Now. Before he hurts someone."

"But Mr. Bingle, he's flying, in the warehouse. You've got to come see. You're kill…killing him… murder…murderer…MURDERER!"

The guards began to drag Coleman down the hallway and descended on the escalator, winding their way through Women's Shoes and Cosmetics.

Even Miss Jackson felt a pang of sorrow as she watched her former boss forcibly removed from the store, the stuffed Bingle still clutched in his arms. The wild look in his eyes and the spit rolling down his chin made him look like a madman.

"Poor Mr. Coleman," Miss Jackson said. "He gets all worked up every Christmas, but this time he's completely lost it."

"Girl, that's a shame," said her colleague from the Fragrance Counter. "I heard he ain't been right since his lil' boy died."

"Least not at this time of year." Miss Jackson shook her head. "It's a damn shame."

As the guards dragged Coleman out the Canal Street entrance, he bellowed for all to hear:

"SOMEBODY…PLEASE…HELP…
SAVE…MISTER…BINGLE!"

Chapter 6

"You sure you don't want anything for breakfast, baby?" Berniece Coleman shouted to her husband from the kitchen, as he sat on the living room floor in front of the Christmas tree wearing his pajamas, bathrobe, and slippers.

Coleman didn't even muster a reply. He didn't have the energy. A blank look in his eye, he stared at the pieces of train track scattered around him, trying to recall how they fit together, even though he'd performed the ritual every Christmas for the last forty years. He felt like he was looking at the pieces of his broken life, desperately searching for a way to put them all back together.

He'd been this way for two days straight. Didn't want to see anybody. Didn't want to talk to anybody. He'd gone so far as to unplug the phone from the wall after it wouldn't stop ringing. Prob-ably con-cerned coworkers wanting to try and lift his spirits. He didn't want any help. He'd been down before, and experience told him he'd rather be left alone to work through it. When he was ready, he'd talk.

"How 'bout a sandwich?" Berniece said. "It's almost lunch anyway." She rounded into the room, dressed in a smart purple pants suit, her matching handbag draped over her arm. A retail veteran herself, Berniece was headed out for the day's shift at Saks Fifth Avenue in Canal Place.

Coleman grunted an unintelligible verdict.

"Well you just gonna' sit there and pout all day?" she said. Coleman fired back an injured look. Berniece shook her head and opened the front door, exiting momentarily and returning with the day's newspaper. "Plenty other stores would hire you in a heartbeat, 'Wood? You just got to pick yourself up and put yourself back together."

She walked over and set the paper in his lap. Coleman looked up at her like a sad puppy, causing Berniece to drop to one knee and try to offer a hug.

"It's gonna' be okay, baby," she said. But Coleman was having none of it. Still reeling from his disturbing hallucinations, his humiliating expulsion from the store, and his sadness over the demise of a fluffy, white snow fairy, he feared he was on the verge of a psychotic break. He wasn't sure he should be touching *anyone* anytime soon.

Coleman pushed Berniece away, drawing a frown and a sharp response. "Fine. If you gon' be like that." She kissed him on the forehead and stood up. "I gotta' go. Maybe you can find something in the classifieds. Call me if you need anything. You know where I'll be. Love you."

Coleman finally looked up to see his wife closing the door behind her. "Love you."

He sighed, abandoning his train set and unfolding the paper. Ordinarily, he would head straight to the Sports section, but something on the front page of Metro caught his eye: his name.

The headline read:

Fillmore's Manager Implicated in Bingle Plot

The subhead:

Disgruntled employee planned doll's demise

Coleman felt sick to his stomach as he read the first paragraph:

A department store manager plotted to "kill" Mr. Bingle, Marigny Brothers' popular Christmas mascot, in order to express dissatisfaction with the company's recent takeover by Fillmore's Department Stores, company management said Tuesday.

The second paragraph was worse:

Haywood Coleman, 47, of New Orleans, a 25-year veteran of Marigny Brothers, allegedly masterminded a series of high-profile accidents involving Mr. Bingle in order to tarnish the store's image among local consumers.

It was only downhill from there:

"Fillmore's Department Stores has uncovered evidence that Mr. Coleman was directly responsible for the recent, unfortunate events involving Mr. Bingle," said Willard Fillmore III, Fillmore's District Manager, in a prepared

statement.

"Mr. Coleman's actions were premeditated and were intended to ruin Christmas for the children and families of New Orleans, but most importantly, to ruin Christmas for Fillmore's and its many loyal patrons. We have since terminated Mr. Coleman, and we have strongly urged that he seek professional counseling."

Despite repeated calls to his home, Coleman could not be reached for comment at press time.

Fillmore would not divulge the details of the conspiracy, but he did allude to Mr. Bingle's spectacular fall from a helicopter over Canal Street as well as an on-camera fire during his daily televised puppet show.

"Because of the financial and emotional distress caused by these incidents," Fillmore said, "Fillmore's will be removing Mr. Bingle from its stores for the duration of this holiday season."

Fillmore did not specify whether Mr. Bingle would return next year, although he did say that a replacement character, Johnny Winter, would take Mr. Bingle's place indefinitely.

Coleman tossed the paper down and buried his head in his hands. He couldn't fathom what was happening. Not only had Fillmore plotted to get rid of Mr. Bingle, but now he was trying to pin all the blame on someone who was unable to defend himself.

Coleman cast his eyes up to the ceiling and

shouted to the God that so often seemed to torment
him. "Why are you doing this to me?"

He rolled onto his knees, then slid forward to
rest his weight on his elbows. The pain welled in
his chest, and he began to sob.

"Why?" he screamed into the carpet. "Why?"

Coleman wanted to cry out against all the
injustice that had been heaped upon him, against all
the injustice in the world. Any world in which evil
men succeeded while honest men suffered was not a
world that Coleman wanted to inhabit. He wanted
to say so much, but there was so much to say. The
glut of words in his mouth resulted in nothing more
than a guttural bellow.

"Unnffuggghhh." His chest heaved, and his
back arched as he lay on the floor. His mind flashed
to the handgun stashed in the drawer of his bedside
table. He would run grab it if he had the energy, but
all his might was directed toward cursing the
heavens. He began pounding his fist, feeling the
reverberations across the floor. The pulsing rhythm
seemed to resonate throughout the house and had a
soothing effect. He beat the carpet until his arm
grew tired, and when he stopped he noticed that the
pounding continued.

He lifted his head from his quasi-fetal position.
The pounding he'd heard all along was coming
from the front door. He had a visitor.

The realization stunned him into silence, and his
anguish dissipated in a heartbeat. He stood slowly

and peered toward the door, uncertain whether or not he should answer. He was in no condition to receive visitors. Surely, whoever it was would leave. But the knocking continued. Maybe they'd heard him.

Coleman lifted his arm and wiped his eyes with the terry-cloth robe. He heard a muffled voice coming from the other side of the door. It sounded like a woman's. "Mr. Coleman? Mr. Coleman."

He stepped toward the door and leaned forward to peek through the peephole. On the other side, he saw a young woman who looked vaguely familiar.

"Who is it?" Coleman said.

"Hope Lawson, *Daily Doubloon*."

Coleman's knees went weak. He scrambled over to the newspaper and looked at the byline on his story. Hope Lawson, one and the same.

"Mr. Coleman, I'd like to ask you some questions," the voice said. "Please, this will just take a few minutes."

Coleman ripped open the door, scowling. He waved the newspaper in his hand. "How come you ain't called me before you wrote this garbage? Why you want to do a brother like that?"

Lawson threw up her hands in defense. "I'm sorry, Mr. Coleman, we've been trying to contact you for the past two days, but we can't get through on the phone. That's why I'm here now."

Coleman cast a glance at the phone cord lying on the ground next to the jack on the wall. He shrugged. "Yeah, well, that don't give you permission to print lies without making sure they're true."

"Sir, I understand. Like I said, that's why I'm here, to get your side of the story."

Coleman took a step back so he could size up his guest. He saw from her body language that she was telling the truth. He waved her inside to an armchair opposite the sofa. She took a seat and prepared a tape recorder and notepad, while he straightened the scattered sections of newspaper.

"I knew something about Willard Fillmore's story didn't add up by the way he was being so secretive," she said. "He said he had evidence of your involvement in this plot, but he wouldn't share any of it with me. Said it would reveal important trade secrets."

"Everything that man said is a lie," Coleman said, waving the paper. "There ain't nothing in here true. He's the one behind killin' Bingle."

"I know, I know."

"Then why you ran the story?" Coleman nearly jumped up from his spot on the sofa.

"Look I'm just a reporter. I write the stories my editor tells me to write. And if our biggest advertiser wants thirty-six column-inches to spin this Bingle fiasco, they're going to get it."

"But that ain't how it's supposed to work."

"That's how it works in the real world."

"But in the real world you ruin real people's lives. Ruin them with lies."

"I swear I didn't know that then. I promise. But this morning, I got a call from a guy named Blanchard, Mel Blanchard. Do you know him?"

"No. Should I?"

"If you were behind that helicopter stunt you should. He was the pilot for Offshore Helicopters. It's a one-man operation, really. Poor guy says he'd been out of work since the oil bust. Says he knew the Fillmore family from his wildcatting days back in Texas. Says Fillmore called him at midnight, Thanksgiving night, and offered him five grand cash to fly in Bingle."

"I knew it."

"He says Fillmore gave him specific instructions to drop Mr. Bingle in the middle of Canal Street, but to make it look like an accident. But once the FBI got involved, things got messy. Now Fillmore's hung him out to dry, and Blanchard's going to lose his license and maybe go to jail."

"So now he's gonna' sing so he can save his sorry ass."

"Sort of. Unfortunately, he doesn't have any proof. And given his precarious position, we'd need corroborating evidence."

"Ha. You didn't need no corroborating evidence when that lyin' fool Fillmore come to you."

"Look, Mr. Coleman, again, I apologize. But I'm here to make it right. I want to get a full statement from you."

"But I'm emotionally unstable," he said,

pointing to the quote in the paper. "I need counseling. See? You said it yourself."

"I didn't say that. Mr. Fillmore said it." Lawson felt especially bad about that one. She'd done a search on Coleman and found the death notice for his son, Reginald. About five years earlier. He'd succumbed to sickle cell anemia after years of struggle. He was only twelve.

"My story ain't no better than that pilot's. We both got an axe to grind."

"Well, maybe if you could come up with some kind of documentation. Invoices? Receipts? Bank statements? Any kind of paper trail?"

Coleman's brow furrowed in thought. "I wish I could help you, Miss Lawson, but I ain't got…" His eyes widened, and a smile spread across his face.

"Got what?" she said, hanging on his words. "What is it? Tell me."

"The Bingle memo," Coleman said, slowly, as the revelation illuminated his mind.

"The Bingle memo?"

"The Bingle memo," he said. "You ever use email, Miss Lawson?"

"Oh yeah, we just got it at the paper. It's the greatest thing since the fax machine. But what's that got to do with the Bingle memo?"

"Fillmore always said I should get into the habit of checking my email more regularly." He smiled. "For once, I'm inclined to agree."

Chapter 7

Coleman didn't pretend to sleep, instead
camping on the sofa in front of the television until
Berniece went upstairs to bed. Two hours later, he
was out the door and heading down to the store.

Twenty-five years on the job had given him
intimate knowledge of the hundred-year-old
Marigny Brothers building, with all its eccentric
alcoves, curious crannies, and secret entryways. It
didn't hurt that, in the haste to remove Coleman
from the premises, Fillmore had neglected to take
the man's keys or change locks and security codes.

Besides, in a worst-case scenario, if Coleman
were to encounter Roy or Wayne or whoever was
working security that night, he doubted there would
be any problem – he'd hired them all and knew
their habits from years of scanning security video.
Regardless of who was working, by 1 a.m., the
night watchman would have just finished his
midnight snack and be drifting off for a catnap.

Coleman slid his key into the lock of the
Iberville Street door and slipped inside, proceeding

immediately to the keypad on the wall and entering the security code. He punched in a numerical sequence that would show Willard Fillmore III as having entered the building at 1:03 a.m. Considering Coleman had created and assigned the codes, he knew them all by heart.

Once the beeping of the alarm sensor had ceased, Coleman stood motionless for a minute, listening for the sounds of movement, to see if his presence had been detected. He didn't hear a thing.

He climbed the back staircase that led to the management offices and shuffled down the hallway. Entering his former office with no resistance, he closed the door and turned on the desk lamp.

Coleman sat down and powered up his computer, nervously drumming his fingers on the desk while the machine rebooted. In seconds, a blinking cursor appeared on the screen, followed by a row of software icons.

Coleman double-clicked on his email icon and waited to retrieve the Bingle memo from his In Box, while the dial-up modem emitted a series of ear-piercing clicks, twiddles, and screeches.

Finally, a new window popped up and posed the troubling question, "Would you like to create a new mailbox?"

Coleman replied in the negative and grumbled. He maneuvered the mouse around the screen, searching in vain for his mailbox.

I hate these stupid machines!

He clicked himself in software circles, following one path to a dead end, then trying another. Nothing seemed to work. The more he clicked, the more confused he became. He couldn't understand. Of course, he'd never paid close attention to the intricate workings of the program.

"Dammit!" he cursed in a loud whisper. He started to beat his fist atop his desk but then caught himself. Coleman sat back in his chair and looked around the shadowy room. All of his papers had been shoveled into a box lying beside the desk. He rifled through the documents, hunting for the memo, but he knew it wasn't there. It was trapped inside that plastic and metal mechanical vault, floating around in the ether just out of reach.

Coleman stared across the digital divide, realizing he'd become the unwitting victim of technological progress. Then it hit him.

He sprung from his chair and bolted across the hall, listening again for footsteps before inserting his master key into the lock on Fillmore's office door. He scooted inside and sat down at the computer, quickly booting the machine. He double-clicked on the email icon and, after another modem cacophany, opened Fillmore's personal email box without any resistance.

Live by the sword, die by the sword.

Coleman scrolled through the In Box but couldn't find anything of relevance. That didn't make sense.

Wait. Fillmore sent the Bingle Memo. It would be in his Sent Box.

Coleman had learned at least that much from the manual. He clicked the icon and searched the old messages, one by one, until he found it: Fillmore's memo outlining the plan to eliminate Mr. Bingle. While it contained no incriminating evidence of a conspiracy by Fillmore to stage the recent accidents, it did prove that the impetus to retire Bingle came from senior management and *not* from Coleman. If he could prove Fillmore had lied about this, it would pave the way for further inquiry and, hopefully, clear his name.

A second email, however, did contain the smoking gun he was seeking in the form of a spreadsheet. Coleman clicked open the attachment and studied the rows of numbers. It was the weekly financial report that was sent to company headquarters. Only this one was markedly different than the report that Coleman had prepared by hand just days earlier. Particularly the line item showing Miscellaneous Expenses for holiday decorations.

Found it!

Coleman knew the bloated expense numbers had to have a correlation in the physical world, probably a check that had been cut. He glanced at the file cabinet and grabbed a pair of scissors off the desk. He jammed a blade into the crevice of the locked cabinet drawer and began prying it upward. With the precision of a surgeon, he positioned the blade against the drawer latch and then gave it a hearty whack with the heel of his hand.

The thundering boom from the large metal cabinet echoed throughout the office, but the drawer popped open quietly. Even in the minimal light, Coleman could see there were only a handful of files. No Bingle file. No Special Projects file. But at the rear of the pack was a green folder bearing the name of Fillmore's new mascot, Johnny Winter.

Coleman grabbed it and began to inspect its contents, but something caught his attention. Not a noise but a sensation. The dull thud of heavy footsteps. Judging by the resonance of the vibrations, Coleman figured it must be Big Wayne on duty. Big Wayne. Big Wayne didn't do anything fast, but he was methodical.

Coleman slipped the file inside his shirt and peered out the office door. All clear. He raced back to the computer and forwarded the emails to the address that Hope had given him. Coleman then sprinted across the hall to his old office just as Big Wayne made his way to the top of the stairs.

"Hey!" Big Wayne shouted, detecting a figure slithering through the darkness. "Hey you! Stop right there!"

Big Wayne drew his gun and shouted into his radio. "Clarence, we got a break-in in Sector Four. Give me backup immediately."

Coleman scanned the office for a way out. Who was he kidding? There was no other way out. He was trapped. He felt Big Wayne's labored footsteps drawing closer. Coleman could make a run for it. He could easily outrun the stout young man. But what about Clarence? He was Laurel to Big Wayne's Hardy. He could already hear Clarence sprinting up the back stairs. He was stuck.

"I know you in there," Big Wayne said. "I got a gun here, so don't try anything stupid. Just step out where I can see you." Even though he moved at a snail's pace, he was out of breath.

As Coleman's office came into view, Big Wayne saw that the door was ajar. Clarence bounded down the hall and was quickly at his side. With a nod to his partner, Big Wayne prepared to kick the door open. But as he lifted his foot, Coleman clicked on the light and stepped into the doorway holding a box.

"Mr. Coleman!" Big Wayne and Clarence said in unison.

"Evening, boys."

"Mr. Coleman, you know you ain't supposed to be here," Big Wayne said. "You 'bout scared us half to death." He put his gun back into its holster, then rested his hands on his knees, trying to regain his breath.

"I'm glad to see y'all are on the ball. Mr. Fillmore would be proud." Coleman shifted the heavy box from one arm to the other.

"You know we could have you arrested," Clarence said. "Mr. Fillmore said you're not allowed on the property."

"Come on, Clarence," Coleman said. "You mean to tell me you're not gonna' allow a brother to come and get his own personal belongings?"

Clarence shrugged.

"Especially after y'all already kicked me out and made a fool of me in front of the entire staff?"

"I heard about that," Big Wayne said. "Man, that wasn't right, what they did you like that."

"I'm sorry," Clarence said, relaxing a bit. "You know how it is around here since that boy Fillmore showed up. Gotta' be watchin' your back, else you get your ass fired."

"You think I don't know that?" Coleman said. "They made me out to look like a criminal. Shoot, I gotta' break in just to get my own stuff back. After twenty-five years. You feelin' me? I said twenty-five years. Can't be disrespecting a man like that."

"No indeed," Big Wayne said.

"True. True," Clarence said.

Coleman leaned in close to gain their confidence. "So look, boys, I'm just gonna' go out that back door the way I came in. Gonna' take my stuff home and be out y'all's hair. And we're gonna' forget this ever happened."

"What happened?" Big Wayne said.

"I ain't seen nothing," Clarence said.

The three men began laughing.

"Yeahyouright," Coleman said. He began walking down the hall with his box, while the Johnny Winter file tucked underneath his shirt scratched at his chest.

***

Hope Lawson hadn't been this excited about a story since the day she witnessed a city councilman being carjacked outside his daughter's wedding at Mater Dolorosa Church.

She'd covered more than her share of murders and other heinous crimes, but this one was different. In a world of throwaway journalism, this story had a certain intangible *gravitas*. This story, as they say, had legs. She hoped it would finally be her ticket out of Metro and into a plum assignment in Features.

That's why the messages in her In Box sent her into the stratosphere. It was the Bingle memo, sent at 1:17 a.m. according to the notation, along with a second, more cryptic message that contained some kind of spreadsheet. Lawson wasn't particularly adept at math, which is why she'd majored in Journalism at LSU in the first place. But she knew these numbers meant something. Or else Haywood Coleman wouldn't have sent them.

She began reading the memo.

Dear Fillmore's Manager:

We regretfully announce the retirement of a New Orleans Christmas icon, Mr. Bingle.

One paragraph in, she began formulating the lead for her next story. Having already received the go-ahead from her editor, she couldn't wait to start writing.

In a development directly contradicting statements made to the Daily Doubloon *Tuesday, this newspaper has learned that management of Fillmore's Department Stores engaged in a systematic campaign to eliminate its popular Christmas mascot, Mr. Bingle, in order to replace it with a new, scientifically designed doll.*

Furthermore, according to internal company documents obtained by this newspaper, Fillmore's District Manager, Willard Fillmore III, plotted to stage a series of spectacular accidents involving Mr. Bingle and then place the blame on long-time store manager Haywood Coleman, whom Fillmore recently fired.

Lawson had to shake herself and allow the facts to catch up with her version of the story. Like a savvy sportswriter who crafts an account of the big game while it's still in progress, Lawson had mastered the art of building the outline and filling in the details as they unfolded. In order to meet tight deadlines on late-breaking news, this practice was as common as it was imperative.

But she didn't have to wait long for this story to evolve. Haywood Coleman walked into the expansive newsroom just as she'd opened up the spreadsheet attachment and begun her futile attempt to decipher the lines of numbers. Thankful at the sight, Hope waved him over to her desk.

"Oh good," he said, seeing the email, "I'm glad you got that. I wasn't sure if it went through. I was in kind of a hurry."

Hope looked up from the screen. "I got it," she said, "even though I don't know what it is."

Coleman dropped a file folder on her desk. "Well maybe this will help explain it."

She flipped through the folder's contents, trying to process all the information. Coleman could see she was struggling to make sense of it all. He circled the desk to look over her shoulder.

"See this expense line here?" he said, pointing to a bloated number on the computer screen. "That amount is five thousand dollars more than in the very same report I filed two days earlier."

He sorted through the papers on her desk and produced what looked like a check stub.

"Now you see this? Here's a stub for a five-thousand-dollar check made out to Cash. Only you can see that it was hand-drawn, not computer-generated like most of our checks. This had to be the payment to Offshore Helicopters."

Hope nodded but remained hesitant. "Okay, I get that. But it doesn't prove Fillmore tried to destroy Mr. Bingle. What else do you have?"

Coleman leaned down and shuffled through

more papers. "Well look at this," he said, producing an invoice from Han-Shin Manufacturing in the Guadong Province of China. "This here shows the company paid another five thousand dollars to design and manufacture the Johnny Winter proto-type. And you can see that he tried to bury this expense in the marketing budget." Coleman slid his finger across another column on the on-screen spreadsheet. "And I know *that* number wasn't there in the report I filed."

Hope exhaled heavily, feeling the pressure of a big story mounting. She knew she needed more in order for this to be a slam dunk.

"This is great and all," she said, "but it's still circumstantial. Do you have anything else?"

Coleman scowled, growing impatient with her lack of appreciation for his sleuth work. He slid another document in front of her.

"This looks like an expense report," Hope said.

"It is an expense report."

Hope leaned closer to the page.

"So far as I can tell, it's for three strippers, two emergency flares, and a bottle of Everclear."

"Exactly," Coleman said. "I always knew they were hos. Talkin' 'bout Santa's Playmates. Ha! And them flambeaux? Road flare, bottle of Everclear, and a stuffed animal's like a mirliton cocktail."

"Molotov," Hope said. "Molotov cocktail."

"What's that?"

"Molotov cocktail. Like a Molotov cocktail."

"Girl, I hear that. This *is* cause for celebration." Coleman put up his palm for a high five. Hope slapped his hand, just as a tired looking man with a slight paunch and wrinkled blue shirt approached the desk. The man's shoulders sagged, and he seemed troubled.

"Haywood, I'd like you to meet my editor, Shelly Grubman," Hope said.

Coleman reached out and shook his hand enthusiastically. "Oh, it's a pleasure to meet you, sir. I want to thank you for helping me set the story straight on this Bingle deal."

"Well, don't thank me just yet," Grubman said.

"Yes sir, you bet I'm going to thank you. Fillmore's caused nothing but trouble since he came to town. But we're gonna' fix that."

Grubman sighed and shrugged. "Well, it looks like Mister Fillmore is causing more trouble."

Hope shot up from her seat. "What do you mean 'more trouble'?"

"I just got out of a meeting with Alton," Grubman said, referring to the paper's ancient publisher, Alton Lafourcade. "We've sold a last-minute, two-page ad spread, and he's cutting thirty-six inches off the news budget."

"So?" Hope said, not making any attempt to hide her challenge to Grubman's authority.

"So, I'm cutting your story."

"Aww, come on, Shelly," Hope said. "This story is front-page news. This is huge. Cut something off the wire reports."

"It's not that simple."

"Of course it is," Hope said. "The only way I could possibly imagine there being a problem with my story is if Willard Fillmore's the one…"

The realization sunk in.

"…buying the ad," Grubman said.

"But you can't do that. What about the wall between advertising and editorial?"

"It only exists in theory. Fillmore's is our number one advertiser, especially during Christmas. Revenue's been down. We've got to make our quarterly number." Grubman's words carried the fatigue of one who'd gone up against the Powers That Be and lost one too many times to care anymore. He accepted these kinds of decisions as part of ordinary business.

But Hope Lawson didn't.

"Well that stinks, Shelly. I'm disgusted."

"I'm sorry, Hope. I really am."

"What's he saying, Miss Lawson?" Coleman said, as though he needed a translator. He turned to Grubman. "Please, sir, you've got to run my story. Please. People are gonna' be sending me hate mail for killing Bingle. I ain't gonna' be able to find another job. Please."

Grubman's head dropped. He was unable to look the man in the eye. Coleman turned to Hope like she had some kind of mystical power. "Please, Miss Lawson, you've got to do something."

"I'm going in to talk to Alton about this," she said to Grubman, a veiled threat in her voice.

"Fine. Go ahead," Grubman said. "But he's standing firm on this. It's a done deal."

"I don't care," she said. "This is wrong."

"Hope, are you sure you want to do this?" Grubman said. "We still have that open spot in Features. You go to Alton and you could be kissing your career goodbye, at least at this paper."

Hope looked at Coleman, knowing she had to fix this mess she'd created. "Would you like to accompany me?"

Coleman smiled. "Lead the way."

Chapter 8

"Oscar, there's a man here to see you."

The feeble puppeteer looked up from the half-eaten sandwich in his lap and addressed Phan, his young Vietnamese apprentice, in his usual crotchety tone.

"Ehhh?" Oscar said in a phlegmy wheeze. He was perched atop the five-foot-high scaffolding, from which he worked his magic.

"A man here for you," Phan said, motioning to the front of the Marigny Brothers stage. "A black man. He say it important."

"Important, huh? Is it more important than my lunch? I need to keep my strength up. I got three shows this afternoon."

"He say it about his son. He need your help."

Oscar saw a well-dressed young man hovering behind Phan and grew chastened. "Yes, well then," he said, as he climbed down.

Haywood Coleman stepped into the cramped, backstage area, which was dominated by a dizzying array of Mr. Bingle puppets, all sporting different outfits – sweaters, vests, even a Saints jersey.

"I'm sorry to bother you, Mr. Eisenberg," Coleman said. "My name's Haywood Coleman. I work in Men's Shoes." Despite having worked at the store for more than a decade, Coleman didn't know much about the enigmatic puppeteer who gave life to Mr. Bingle.

The cantankerous old man kept to himself and rarely spoke to anyone unless it was through the puppet. And when he wasn't performing, he huddled like a hermit in his dark, dingy workshop in the back of the store. Catching him out in plain sight was a rare opportunity.

A young boy stood next to Coleman, clutching his hand. Seeing the child, Oscar smiled.

"And who is this?" he said.

"This is my son, Reginald," Coleman said, placing both hands on the boy's shoulders. "He might be Mr. Bingle's biggest fan. He's been coming to see your shows since he was a baby."

"And I got me a Mr. Bingle doll at my house," Reginald added.

"We're on our way to Children's Hospital," Coleman said, "but I promised Reggie I'd take him to see Mr. Bingle first. I forgot you'd be on break. I'm sorry. I'll let you get back to your lunch."

"Nonsense, nonsense," Oscar said. He began wrapping up the uneaten sandwich. "I was just finishing up anyway. I'm saving this half for

Bingle." He winked at Coleman as he tucked the sandwich into his jacket pocket.

Having performed countless shows for ailing children all across southeast Louisiana, Oscar could spot the signs of illness with few, if any, hints. It was in the eyes: a deep and profound fear, an absence of hope. The look broke Oscar's heart every single time he witnessed it. But it inspired him to give his all, to offer what little he could to salvage a child's spirit.

"I'll tell you what," Oscar said. "Reginald, if you'll go back out to the foot of the stage, I'll ask Mr. Bingle if he can spare a few minutes. How's that sound?"

The boy's eyes lit up. Reginald looked to his father for approval, and Coleman nodded.

"And here, take one of these," Oscar said, holding out a peppermint candy cane. "Can't have Christmas without a candy cane." Again, Reginald looked to Coleman.

"Go on. It's okay," Coleman said. Reginald smiled and snatched the candy. Then, in a heart-beat, the boy was sitting at the edge of the stage.

"Thank you," Coleman said. He reached for Oscar's hand and shook it vigorously. "This will mean so much to him. Thank you."

"Don't mention it," Oscar said. He leaned closer. "Between you and me, what's wrong?"

"Sickle cell anemia," Coleman said. "Been in and out of hospitals his whole life."

"Poor kid."

"Doctor says he might have to stay through Christmas again."

"That's a shame. It pains my heart, it really does."

"At this point, I'm just marking time by holidays," Coleman said, "prayin' he'll live to see Christmas, then Mardi Gras, then who knows."

"I hear that." Oscar fell into a fit of coughing. After a moment, he recovered and posed an odd question. "Tell me, does he still believe?"

Coleman sighed. "I don't know. I don't think he believes in much of anything any more. Probably gets it from his old man."

Oscar picked up a Mr. Bingle puppet and prepared to ascend the scaffolding. "Well, let's see what we can do about that."

Coleman stepped to the front of the stage and watched Mr. Bingle come into view. The puppet's high-pitched voice boomed through the speakers on each side of the stage.

"Hello little boy, what's your name?"

Reginald scurried closer to the puppet and regarded him like he would the Easter Bunny or the Tooth Fairy or, yes, even Santa Claus. An irrepressible smile washed over his face, and he bounced up and down with excitement. "My name's Reginald. And I know you. You're Mr. Bingle!"

Coleman marveled at the sight of his son

carrying on a conversation with the puppet. Other shoppers gathered around to watch Bingle and Reginald, and children begged their parents for an opportunity to speak one-on-one with the little white fairy.

"Tell me, Reginald, do you still believe in Santa Claus?" Mr. Bingle asked.

Reginald cast his eyes downward and his shoulders drooped. "I don't know."

Oscar tried to maintain a playful tone. "Don't know? What do you mean you don't know? Of course you still believe in Santa Claus. You still believe in me, don't you?"

Reginald perked up. "Well yeah, but…"

"But what?"

"But every year, when I tell Santa what I want, he don't bring it. Even if I been good."

Bingle's little mitten covered his mouth. "He doesn't bring it. Oh my!"

Oscar knew he had a tricky situation here.

"Well, what are you asking for?" Bingle said.

"I ask him to take away my sick cell."

"Your what?"

"My sick cell," Reginald said. "That's what make me sick all the time. I ask him to take it away. Instead, he brings me toys and junk. How I'm supposed to believe in Santa Claus if he don't bring me what I ask for?"

Coleman held his breath. This exchange was not turning out the way he had hoped. He suddenly wished Oscar had not been so accommodating. Why couldn't he have just put on a little show like he did for all the other kids? Instead, by removing the wall between performer and audience, he had exposed painful truth of reality. The magic of the fantasy was destroyed.

Or was it?

"Reginald, I'm afraid that Santa Claus can't take away your sickle cell," Mr. Bingle said.

Alarm shot through Coleman's body as he watched his boy react to the news.

What was this nutty old man doing?

"He can't?" Reginald said, the disappointment evident.

"No, he can't. Only you can. If you believe."

Reginald's voice rose in wonder. "Really?"

"Really," Bingle said. "And I'll tell you what Santa Claus *can* give you."

"What?"

"He can give you the power to believe."

"Believe? Believe in what?"

"Believe in anything you want," Bingle said. "It's the most powerful force in the world. I'll tell you what I believe. I believe that I'm going to live forever."

"Really?" Reginald's pitch rose higher. "But what if you get old, or sick like me?"

Bingle's little mittens waved through the air. "This old body is like a suit. It'll wear out. Get sick. But your spirit, your spirit lives forever."

Reginald's eyes crinkled. "Do I have a spirit?"

"Of course you do. We all do. Do you want to find it?" Reginald nodded, an earnest look in his eyes.

"Then come here and grab my hand." The boy walked to within arm's reach of the puppet and grabbed one of his tiny mittens. "Now close your eyes…and listen." The boy complied, but it was clear he did not understand, as evidenced by his continuous fidgeting.

"I don't hear anything," Reginald said.

"No, no, no," Bingle said. "You've got to be quiet…and still. *Be still*."

"Be still?"

"Be still, and listen. You'll hear a buzzing in the very deepest part of your heart. And if you listen hard enough, you'll feel it too, a buzzing like a little bumble bee. That's your spirit."

Reginald pressed his eyes together tightly and squeezed Bingle's mitten, remaining quiet and still for the better part of a minute. Coleman watched the tension in his son's face dissipate and a peaceful glow slowly come over him. Eyes still closed, Reginald's mouth opened, and a look of wonder overtook him.

"I feel it. I feel it," he said.

"Shhhhh," Bingle said.

"I feel it," Reginald said again in a whisper.

"We're not finished yet. Be quiet."

Reginald's outburst subsided but his smile

remained. He looked like he'd just received the greatest Christmas gift ever.

Coleman felt so grateful to Oscar that he wanted to run behind the stage and kiss him. He could not rightly tell whether Reginald comprehended that he was talking to a puppet and not an actual living creature. Either way, the boy didn't seem to care.

Perhaps the power of belief was already at work.

***

Since Reginald's death, Coleman had come to dread the night. Endless night. Each trip to bed a dark, mournful sentence.

He would lie awake and replay a thousand memories in his mind, a million questions yet unanswered, a lifetime of fears, doubts, disappointments, missed opportunities, and things left unsaid.

For one so outwardly successful, who'd picked himself up by the bootstraps and lifted himself out of poverty, out of the hopeless pit of the St. Thomas Housing Projects, Haywood Coleman felt like a miserable failure. Where had he gone wrong?

To his right, Berniece slept soundly. She had no trouble sleeping since going on Xanax. Lately, she behaved as if her entire emotional response system was shrouded in a chemical haze. The only feeling she displayed with any conviction, it seemed, was

scorn directed at her husband. Except they were
no longer husband and wife, at least in the spiritual
sense. They were housemates, whose comings and
goings evoked little interest or fanfare from one
another.

Coleman lay on his back with his eyes closed,
reliving the scene in Alton Lafourcade's office from
earlier that day. His visit with Hope had been a
complete waste of time. He could tell from the tone
in the old man's voice the instant he called them in.
Such a cold, stern rebuke from such an elegant
man. How could he have been so callous?

At least Hope was still in Coleman's corner,
having taken personal accountability for his
redemption. Judging by the look on her face when
Lafourcade denied their petition to run the story,
she felt worse than Coleman did. She pledged not to
stop until he was vindicated.

Together, they would take the story to the local
television news media. After all, the *Daily Doubloon* may have been the monopoly daily, but it did
not have a monopoly on the news. Tomorrow
offered promise.

But in the meantime was the night.

Interminable night.

Cold night.

Lonely.

Help me.

The words that crept into Coleman's head
startled him. He'd long since given up asking

anything of the universe. It was a heartless, unfeeling mass of energy, devoid of spirit or humanity. It was his adversary, as events had well proven. He did not need charity, and he did not pray to any god. His strength, he believed, came entirely from within.

Coleman seized control of his thoughts and pictured his trip to the television station in the morning. Certainly, the television media were not beholden to Fillmore's in the same manner as the newspaper. They would lend a sympathetic ear. And if not, then radio.

He rehearsed his pitch to the news editor, crafting his argument and the order in which he would display his corroborating evidence. He would need a visual hook, yes. They'd surely have footage of Bingle's farewell puppet show…and the helicopter fiasco.

Coleman felt his legs getting clammy under the covers, as his heart raced along with his thoughts.

They won't be able to resist this story.

And he'd need a personal hook. He'd need to come off as likeable. Maybe he could hold a Mr. Bingle doll in his arms while he spoke. He still had that old Mr. Bingle doll. Right there on Reginald's bed, same place he'd left it after that sleepwalking incident the other night.

He couldn't gain a clear image of the doll in his mind's eye. He had put it back, hadn't he? Or had Berniece thrown it out? She wouldn't have done that, would she? She wasn't that cold-hearted. No, definitely not. The doll had to be there. But he couldn't see it. He wouldn't be able to rest until he did. He closed his eyes tighter but was unable to focus.

Come on, dammit!

Nothing. Blackness.

Coleman sprung from the bed and padded down the hall. He threw open the door to Reginald's old room and nearly tripped over a stack of boxes just inside the doorway. Old toys. Books from St. Francis Xavier Elementary. He'd just started sixth grade when the last flare-up occurred.

Coleman stepped over the boxes to get to the bed. He flipped over pillows. Pulled down the sheets. Dumped a pile of old clothes from the armchair in the corner. Kicked at a stack of magazines. No Bingle.

He caught himself. If Berniece found him in here she'd think he'd lost it, for sure. Coleman shook his head and prepared to exit the room when a noise from downstairs stopped him cold. He cocked his ear. A train whistle. A rolling swish. Clapping. Laughter.

Coleman raced down the stairs and stood awestruck at the sight: his young son, in pajamas, cheering on the passing train cars. He must have been nine years old.

Reginald!

Sitting astride the engine was none other than

Mr. Bingle, his mitten waving in the air.

The image of Reginald cast a shimmering, golden glow across the room, creating a spark in Coleman's eye. The boy turned to him.

"Look, Daddy," he said, pointing to Bingle and then resuming his wild clapping.

"I see, I see," Coleman said in a quivering voice, slowly descending the final steps and tiptoeing across the floor like he was sneaking up on an intruder. Drawing closer with each step, Coleman prayed the phantom would not flee in fright. Instead, the boy did quite the opposite.

"Look what I did, Daddy," Reginald said, still pointing. "I did this for you."

The train tracks wound around the small, barren tree, which, in happier days, would have been cluttered with presents this time of year.

Coleman sat on the carpet next to Reginald, breathing ever so lightly. He resisted the urge to wrap his arms around his son for fear that he would grasp only air. Failing that, he sat in the golden glow, bathing in the divine light. The warmth of his love for the boy flooded into his heart, and the aching beauty of life itself squeezed tears from the corners of his eyes. Reginald turned to him and smiled.

"Don't cry, Daddy. It's okay."

Coleman sniffled. "But I miss you, boy. I miss you bad." He lifted his hand to touch the boy's hair. He could feel the pulsating heat.

"But I'm still here," Reginald said. "I ain't never left. I got a job to do."

"What are you talking about, Reg?"

"I got a job. To take away the pain from all the lil' children. Only it don't hurt me no more."

"But it still hurts me."

"That's 'cause your heart's closed. When you open your heart, a light shine through." Reginald flashed one of his hundred-thousand-watt smiles. "And it's all good."

Coleman burst into a sniffling laugh.

"But how?"

"You just got to believe, Daddy?"

"But it's hard."

Reginald rolled his eyes. "Na-ah, looka' here." He held out his hand. Coleman lifted his own, ever so cautiously, and touched the warm flesh.

"Coleman?" Berniece called from the stairs.

Coleman didn't reply. He couldn't. His eyes were frozen on Reginald, as he reunited with his long-lost son.

Halfway down the stairs, Berniece caught sight of the vision and gasped. She lifted her hand to cover her mouth. "Oh Lord. Reginald, baby!"

Coleman sat clasping the boy's hand, while Bingle continued his circuitous parade around the tree, arm still waving in the air. Berniece nearly stumbled as she descended the remaining steps.

"Daddy, even though I'm gone, you ain't never alone. Like Mr. Bingle said, your spirit lives forever. We're always here for you, no matter what happens. "

"We?" Coleman said. "What do you mean 'we'?"

Without answering, Reginald reached out with both his arms to pull his father in for a big hug. Coleman closed his eyes and felt himself floating into another realm of existence, a world filled with light and warmth and a continual buzz that called forth his most primitive recollections of the womb. It was a fullness that required no further action. Absolute peace. Bliss.

Was this what heaven felt like?

When his eyes fluttered open again, he was speechless. In his arms, he held Berniece, pressed tightly against his chest. She, too, had given herself over to the vision, and tears ran down her cheeks. They looked at each other and smiled, as the train continued in the background.

"I love you, baby," Coleman said.

"I love you, too," Berniece said.

Together, they continued rocking in each other's arms, bathed once again in love's glow.

Chapter 9

Hope took her reassignment to the Obituary Desk at the newspaper about as well as one could expect. At the very least, it simplified her task when Coleman requested she search the *Daily Doubloon* obit archive for Edwin H. "Oscar" Eisenberg.

Finding Eisenberg's death notice, as well as an accompanying story, Hope's instincts as a reporter went into overdrive. She sensed there was something left untold.

The old puppeteer had been as inscrutable as Mr. Bingle was beloved. Quiet and shy, Oscar seemed to find his voice only when acting through his puppets. As he grew older, his behavior turned erratic and undependable, as was his health. Many legends circulated about his inability to distinguish where he left off and Bingle began.

Forced into retirement by age and illness, Oscar dropped out of sight until his death in the late 1980s. Without any family to care for him or about him, Edwin Harmon "Oscar" Eisenberg died penniless and utterly alone. If not for the largesse of the

Marigny family, he would have been buried in a pauper's grave. As it turned out, Edwin Harmon "Oscar" Eisenberg's fate was not much better.

Hope emerged from her car at the front gates of Eternal Rest #3 Cemetery on Humanity Street and looked for Coleman, hoping she'd find him very quickly. This god-forsaken plot of worthless dirt was tucked away in a forgotten corner of Gentilly, surrounded by rickety shotgun cottages, abandoned warehouses and unused train tracks, overgrown with weeds. The only sound cutting through the air on this damp, December morning was the distant whoosh of cars on I-10.

Hope swung open the rusted, iron gate and stepped inside, immediately feeling the despair of so many inconsequential souls. She was relieved at the sight of Coleman, who appeared outside a squat, caretaker's shack, accompanied by a hobbling old man who wore a green work shirt and a Dobbs cap over his bald head.

"Hope, this is Lloyd Herman," Coleman said. "He runs this place."

The caretaker laughed. "Yeah, right. As you can see, there ain't much runnin' goin' on." He waved his hand across the broad expanse of the cemetery, all low headstones and faded, plastic flowers. Here on the Gentilly ridge was one of the few places in town where you could dispose of bodies in the earth, as opposed to the ornate, above-ground tombs of the city's more famous burial grounds like St. Louis #1, Metairie Cemetery, and Odd Fellow's Rest.

"Y'all the foist visitors we had in about a month," Herman said, leading them down the grassy central pathway. "What, y'all say, ya reporters or something?"

"Well, I am," Hope said.

"I just work at Fillmore's," Coleman said. "Or at least I used to."

Herman sighed. "Aw, it's a shame what they tryin' to do to dat Mr. Bingle, huh? I seen a photo of dat new guy. What's his name, Chucky Winter or somethin' like dat? Look like he got beat wit da ugly stick. Poor Mista Eisenberg's probly' toinin' in his grave. I know I sure would be."

Hope and Coleman walked carefully over the uneven terrain, choosing each step as though they feared waking some restive soul, or, worse, tumbling into a dark abyss. The shifting soil had pitched the burial plots at odd angles, creating the unsettling image of a churning ocean, an angry sea of the dead.

"Mr. Herman's been here thirty-three years," Coleman said to Hope, trying to break the uncomfortable silence.

"Really," Hope said. "Were you here for Mr. Eisenberg's funeral?"

Herman laughed. "Wasn't much of a funeral, if you even wanna' call it dat. There was like three or four people here. Ol' Mista Marigny, before he passed. I think Mista Allen was here – he's da man who dreamt up da Bingle doll. A couple others. You'da thought there'da been more hoopla made about it, but there wasn't. Least not around here. Dey jus' put him in da ground and left."

Coleman fidgeted, wondering if he would ever locate the loose thread he'd been searching for.

"Do you remember if there was anything unusual about the ceremony?" he said. "Anything, I don't know, strange, you know, weird?"

Herman laughed again. "Like I said, it wasn't much of a ceremony. I mean, if ya lookin' for somethin' all mysterious like dat, no, I can't say as there was."

Coleman shot a look to Hope that conveyed his disappointment. But it dissipated as soon as the expedition party came upon the grave.

"Well, here it is," Herman said, gesturing to a patch of dead grass in between two other unassuming grave sites.

"Here's what?" Coleman said.

"Da grave," Herman said.

"Where?" Hope said. All she saw was what looked like a cut-through to the next row of plots.

Herman stamped his foot on the ground and pointed downward. "Right here. I'm practically standin' on it."

"But there's nothing there," Coleman said. He squatted down to run his hand over the grass.

"Dat's what I been tryin' to tell ya," Herman

said. "Wasn't much of nothin'."

"You mean there's not even a marker?" Hope said. "Even the paupers' graves get a stick with some numbers on it so you can look up the file in City Hall. Isn't there anything?"

"Not as long as I been here," Herman said. "No tombstone, no marker, no nothin'. Jus' dirt." Coleman glanced at Hope and felt a jolt through his chest.

Is this what life comes to?

"I don't know what y'all was hopin' to find," Herman said, "but there ain't nothin' much here. A patch of dead grass won't make a very good story."

Hope smiled, knowing the old man was dead wrong. Like so many world-weary souls, Lloyd Herman couldn't discern the profound from the mundane. Surrounded by so much death, he was blind to the sublime glory of life.

"Amazing," Coleman said.

"I think I might cry," Hope said.

"Dawlin', it breaks my hawt," Herman said.

The three stood in silence paying their respects to the dead man. A cool, damp breeze kicked up, carrying the fertile stench of mud and wet grass.

"What does a good headstone cost these days?" Hope said. Herman started to answer, but Coleman cut him off.

"Nice one'll run you fifteen-hundred dollars. Tombstone is about twice that, depending on how elaborate you want to make it."

Hope looked to Herman for confirmation. He nodded, clearly impressed and surprised by Coleman's knowledge of such arcane data.

"Fifteen hundred, huh?" Hope said. "Well, Mr. Herman, thank you for your time. You've been very helpful." Without another word, she turned and began marching back to the car. Coleman followed close behind, comprehending her meaning.

"That's it? That's all y'all wanted?" Herman called out, hobbling in their wake. He finally caught up at the front gate, nearly out of breath.

"Mr. Coleman," he said, "there was one other thing. I almos' forgot."

Coleman and Hope stopped to listen.

"I remember at the funeral, when they was throwin' da dirt back on da grave, there was dis little boy watchin'. I figured he was from da neighborhood, y'know, 'cause dem kids always comin' round here tryin' to spook each other."

Coleman felt the blood draining from his face. Herman took off his hat and scratched his head, smiling in wonder at the memory.

"Yeah, I remember dis little boy, he was a little black boy, and he looked all sad, and he just stood there watchin' till da men finished puttin' da dirt on the coffin. Den when dey was finished, da little boy went over and put somethin' on top of da dirt."

Herman chuckled.

"What was it?" Coleman asked, hanging on the

old man's words.

"It was the strangest thing. I remember, I thought maybe he'd picked some clovers or somethin' and wanted to put some wild flowers on da grave. So I went over and checked it out."

"What was it?" Hope said, also hooked.

"It was a little candy cane. You know, like da one Mr. Bingle held in his left hand. Dat little boy put a candy cane on Mr. Eisenberg's grave. How he knew who was bein' buried there I'll never know. It was just a little black boy from da neighborhood. But he put a candy cane on da man's grave. How bout dat, huh? A candy cane. Dat was really somethin'. Be sure to put dat in ya story."

Coleman felt his heart trying to explode through his chest. He reached out for Hope's shoulder to steady himself. He knew logically that it couldn't have been Reginald. But how many other lives had Eisenberg touched?

"Whoa, there," Herman said. "You okay?" He extended his arms to offer additional support should Coleman need it.

"I'm alright, I'm alright," Coleman said, steadying himself. He smiled. "Never better."

"Scared me there for a second," Herman said.

Hope smiled at Coleman and then at the old man. "We'll be sure to put that in our story."

"Count on it," Coleman said.

***

Poor Phan was at his wit's end over the new Johnny Winter puppet. He'd never made so many kids cry in his life.

He got into this gig to bring smiles not tears. But once Winter's show began, the children couldn't get away fast enough.

His troubles were compounded by the fact that Ray the Drunk had been fired after the TV-show incident. Ever since, Phan had struggled to find a suitable voice for the new puppet, but in the end he came off sounding like Fu Manchu channeling the spirit of Mickey Rooney. From their horrified reactions, you'd have thought the kids were witnessing a crime. And in a sense, they were. Because the children knew – without any adults even saying so – that Johnny Winter's presence meant Mr. Bingle had been stolen from them.

Phan, for one, couldn't take it any longer. He had a reputation to protect. After yet another poorly received show, he took his case to Fillmore.

"Mista Fillmore, it just not working," Phan said. He held the offending puppet in his arms.

"What's not working?" Fillmore said, yanking Johnny Winter from Phan and testing its strings to make sure they were functional. "It looks fine to me." He handed the doll back to Phan.

"No," Phan said, holding the doll upright to illustrate his point. "Look at his face. He scary. He not funny. This is Christmas, not Halloween. I make children cry. I don't like that."

Fillmore refused to give any ground. "Have you ever thought that it might be the puppeteer and not the puppet?" He arched an eyebrow.

"Impossible," Phan said.

"Maybe we just need to look for new talent."

"Maybe you need to look for new doll. I'm not the only one who think so. Those people outside agree with me."

Phan pointed out the store's front window to a line of picketers marching on the Canal Street sidewalk: the Mr. Bingle Fan Club. They waved protest signs and chanted slogans calling for the return of their beloved Mr. Bingle.

"Those people," Fillmore said, a note of disgust in his voice, "are insane."

A protestor caught Fillmore's eye through the window and issued a profane hand gesture.

"Who the hell pickets over a Christmas doll?" Fillmore said.

"Mr. Bingle not just a doll," Phan said, offended. "He's a puppet, too."

"Oh whatever. If they don't clear my sidewalk, I'm going to have them all thrown in jail. This is bad for business."

"*This* bad for business," Phan said, holding up the doll again.

"Are you saying you don't want your job any more? I'm sure there are a few dozen unemployed puppeteers running around who would be glad to take your place…at half the salary."

Phan knew he'd been cornered. He dropped his head. "No."

"Good, then I suggest going back to that creepy workshop of yours and figuring out how to make Chucky Win-...eh, Johnny Winter put smiles on those kids' faces."

As Phan turned to leave, a shower of boos and catcalls caught Fillmore's attention. The ruckus was coming from outside. A dark figure cutting through the picket line had incurred the wrath of this unruly mob. Fillmore's heart leapt. An ally?

He moved closer to investigate, but his hopes were dashed when the target of the taunts came into view. It was Coleman, accompanied by Hope.

"Oh, it's you," Fillmore said.

"Merry Christmas to you, too," Coleman said.

"And who's your little friend?"

"Hope Lawson," Hope said, shaking Fillmore's hand. "We spoke by phone a few days ago."

"She's the reporter at the *Daily Doubloon* you lied to to slander my name," Coleman said.

"I did not..." Fillmore said. He retracted his hand from Hope's, then sneered. "Don't get any ideas, Coleman. I wouldn't bother running to the press with your sob story. Not going to happen."

"We're well aware of that," Hope said.

"But that's not why we're here," Coleman said. "We want to offer you an opportunity."

Fillmore burst into a condescending laugh.

"What could you possibly have to offer?"

"How about a chance to save this store, save Fillmore's reputation, make your quarterly revenue numbers, and make you look like a hero?" Coleman said. "Sound good?"

Fillmore perked up. "Tell me more."

Hope stepped forward. "Well, we've discovered that Oscar Eisenberg, the original puppeteer and voice-man for Mr. Bingle…"

"Oh enough with the Mr. Bingle already," Fillmore said.

"No, wait," Coleman said. "Just hear us out." He signaled Hope to proceed.

"We've discovered that he's buried in an unmarked grave right in the middle of town. There's no tombstone, no headstone, or any other recognition of his contribution to New Orleans culture and history. This is big."

Fillmore stood unfazed. "Yeah, so. He was a puppeteer, for Chrissakes. In my book, that's one step removed from being a derelict. What do you want, to put up a shrine?"

"We were thinking about a campaign," Coleman said, "to tell people Eisenberg's story and raise money for some kind of memorial."

"Like a tombstone," Hope said. "And a commemorative plaque."

"A plaque? A plaque where?" Fillmore said.

"Right outside the store." Coleman pointed to the sidewalk where the picketers were still at it. "You can take full credit for it. You can imagine the groundswell of support for Fillmore's that this will generate."

"All the local media will jump on the story," Hope said. "It's tailor-made for Christmas. Paying tribute to a man's life. Righting a wrong and, in the process…"

"…and in the process," Coleman said, "bringing back Mr. Bingle."

Fillmore laughed again, but this time the look in his eyes showed that the offer had struck a nerve. Coleman sensed the resistance dissolving. He pressed further. "There is one other thing."

"What's that?" Fillmore said.

"I'd want my job back," Coleman said. "And a public acknowledgment of my innocence."

"You don't have to absorb any blame," Hope said, trying to soften Fillmore. "We can do a story saying it was all a big misunderstanding."

"I'll come back to work, and it will all go back to normal, just like it was before all this." Coleman swept his hand to take in the picketers and the store in one broad pass.

"Everybody will be so caught up in the Eisenberg story," Hope said, "they'll forget Bingle was ever in jeopardy, and they'll return to shopping at Fillmore's, just in time for Christmas."

Fillmore batted the proposal back and forth in his mind till it was tattered like a dog's old tennis ball. Recognizing the puppeteer would be a nice gesture for the dead man.

But then Fillmore's would have to acknowledge guilt, even if only implied guilt. But the ploy might boost sales and help him make his numbers.

But that would bring Coleman back into the picture. He couldn't have that. He couldn't work with Coleman, flat-out. He couldn't have a subordinate twenty years his senior constantly questioning his decisions and undermining his authority. No, that was a deal-breaker.

But who's to say he couldn't just take the idea?

And leave Coleman out in the cold.

"Gee, guys, that's a neat idea and all, but I just don't know," Fillmore said.

Coleman had anticipated opposition. Fortunately, he came prepared.

"Or else…," Coleman said.

"Or else what?" The challenge reawakened Fillmore's latent contempt for humanity, which lay dormant but could rise to strike like a viper at a moment's notice. "You can't go to the newspaper. I've already seen to that."

"Or else we can go talk to the television news," Hope said. "Unlike the newspaper, your friends at Channel 6 don't have a monopoly on TV news." Together, they had Fillmore on the run.

Fillmore swallowed hard. He hadn't thought about that. Of course, he didn't think they did real news on TV any more. Just fluff pieces about celebrity scandals, diet fads, and the latest techno-gadgets. Maybe he was wrong. But he couldn't let on. Had to save face.

"Right. Like they're going to believe you." His nervousness cut through his laugh. "Good luck."

The trio stood silent like gunfighters at an old-west standoff.

"We don't need luck," Coleman said. "We have evidence."

"Evidence," Fillmore said. "Evidence of what?"

"That you killed Bingle and set me up for it."

"Is that another threat?"

Coleman leaned closer and lowered his voice. "It's not a threat. It's a promise."

Fillmore felt his heart beating up in his throat. Should he relent? Or should he call Coleman's bluff? He needed to stall for time.

"Well, I'm going to need to think about this," Fillmore said. "There are a lot of considerations."

"I can't wait no longer," Coleman said. "My reputation's at stake. And Christmas is right around the corner. We need an answer now."

Fillmore rolled his lip between his index and middle fingers. They definitely didn't have a class on this in business school. It was all happening so fast. If only he could press the "Pause" button to slow things down. He just needed to get oxygen to his brain. He needed to breathe.

Coleman and Hope looked at each other, concerned by Fillmore's strange mannerisms. He appeared on the verge of hyperventilating.

In the midst of his deliberations, Fillmore

caught the eye of a protestor through the window, and, as if in slow motion, the middle-aged woman flashed yet another profane gesture. Just what Fillmore needed to help get his thoughts in order.

His ire revived, Fillmore smiled, although he had lost all capability of making a rational decision.

"You need an answer, huh?" he said, the color having returned to his face.

"That's what I said," Coleman said. Outside, he could hear the picketers launching into another chorus of their protest mantra, *"Jingle, jangle, jingle, bring back Mr. Bingle."*

"Fine. If you want an answer, I've got one. Your answer is no."

Chapter 10

Coleman didn't know whether to take Fillmore's rebuff as a setback or a victory. The only thing he knew for certain was that he had to press on with his fight to save Mr. Bingle.

Despite his tenuous on grip on reality, despite his unsettling visions, and even despite his lack of gainful employment, Coleman felt secure in his course of action. By preserving the little doll and by honoring Oscar Eisenberg, he somehow sensed he would make peace with the loss of Reginald and lay his son to rest for good.

Coleman wasn't merely trying to save Mr. Bingle. He was trying to save himself.

And with Berniece now squarely behind him, he found renewed strength to continue. Armed with a clever plan, a handful of snapshots from Eternal Rest #3, his lucky Bingle doll, and a rickety easel he'd dug out of his garage, Coleman tossed together a visual presentation that would illustrate Eisenberg's saga for the television news media.

Setting up camp on the wide, flagstone sidewalk outside Fillmore's main entrance – directly opposite the Salvation Army's red-kettle bell-ringer – Coleman quickly made his case before the assembled throng of Bingle fans and won them over with Oscar Eisenberg's tale of woe.

Donations poured into his collection basket so briskly that he feared he'd be a target for one of the many thieves who plied their craft on these streets.

"Thank you, ma'am," Coleman said, nodding graciously as a woman dropped a crisp dollar bill into the wicker basket at his feet. He squatted down to collect the money, which was being whipped by a swirling wind like ping pong balls in a bingo machine. He patted the bills into a neat wad and folded it into his pocket.

Better keep the basket from looking too full. Don't want to discourage contributions.

The officer from the Salvation Army cast an envious glance over at Coleman.

"Quite a little racket you got goin' there, Haywood," the officer said.

"Easiest money I ever made, George," Coleman replied, smiling. George Lewis had manned this doorway for the Salvation Army every Christmas for the past seventeen years.

"I'm sorry to hear about your misfortune," George said. "I would say I hope things turn around for you, but from the look of theings, they already are."

Coleman stood upright and repositioned the

basket between his feet.

"Tell you what, G," Coleman said, checking his watch. "I'll be feelin' a whole lot better once them TV cameras get here. It's almost time for the five o'clock news."

George lifted his head to acknowledge a young woman approaching at a brisk pace.

"Looks like they're here now."

Coleman turned to find Hope, and, despite his success, he couldn't hide his anxiety.

"Girl, where have you been? And where are the TV people?"

"Relax, Haywood, they're on their way," Hope said. "They got caught up at City Hall. Paramedics had to be called into the city council meeting."

"Protestors getting out of hand again?"

"No, the mayor was demonstrating his new citywide fitness program. People were dropping like flies. But don't worry, the TV crews will all be here in a minute."

Hope made a quick inspection of Coleman's art project. It would have made any seventh grader proud. "Looks good." Mounted on foam-core board were two photos of Isentrout's grave, accompanied by a photocopied news story on Mr. Bingle that she'd found in the newspaper archives.

The crude-but-effective storyboard conveyed the bare facts of the case. At the top of the presentation, written in large black Marks-A-Lot, were the words "Please Help." She looked down at the empty collection basket.

"It's okay," she said. "Once the story hits, things will pick up."

"Oh, I ain't worried," Coleman said, thumping the wad of bills bulging in his jacket pocket. "We already had to clean it out once. Can't be lookin' too rich when you beggin' for money."

In the crisp, orange glow of the evening sunlight, as the last soothing rays of the day reflected off the tall buildings along Canal Street, Coleman began to feel as though his fortunes had, indeed, turned for the better. A warm sense of well-being washed over him, and he relaxed.

"Anything I can do to help?" Hope said.

"Nah. You've already done plenty," Coleman said. Hope stood with her arms crossed, shifting her weight from right foot to left. Accustomed to being in constant motion, she could not bear even a minute of idle time. Coleman recognized her dis-comfort. "Well, if you really want to help…here." He peeled off a small stack of brightly colored handbills that he'd been giving out to passersby. "You can help me give these out."

"Perfect."

With Coleman manning the collection basket, Hope was able to weave her way through the heavy pedestrian traffic and lure an ever widening spec-trum of donors. The presentation seemed to possess a magnetic power that pulled people into its orbit. Hope had never excelled at sales in any form, but this was easy. And fun. Everyone wanted to help!

With only minutes to spare before the first newscast of the day, a vehicular clamor cut through the air. Initially, Coleman was relieved. But when he saw the source, panic gripped his chest.

"Police?" he said. "What are they doing here?"

Two uniformed patrolmen hopped from the car and immediately set about dispersing the Mr. Bingle protestors from the sidewalk. The rag-tag collection of elderly men, middle-aged women, housewives, and young children (who'd been dragged along to learn the finer points of civil disobedience) put up a weak fight. To be fair, the protestors had been at it since morning and were already planning to call it a day.

On the far side of the horde about twenty yards in the distance, Coleman could see his nemesis, Fillmore, standing at the store entrance, berating the officers in his usual antagonistic fashion.

Seconds later, the lawmen were harassing George from the Salvation Army.

"Not him!" Fillmore called out. He waggled his finger at Coleman.

"Excuse me, sir, can we please see your fund-raising permit?" said an officer, whose nametag read "Jones."

Jones' partner, Officer Cruz, glanced down at the collection basket, which was, again, half-full of crumpled dollar bills and assorted coins.

Coleman frowned. He searched his pockets for a document he knew didn't exist. His hands passed over the bulging money wad in his jacket. Definitely didn't want to hand that over.

"I'm sorry, Officer," Coleman said, "we ain't got one yet." He laughed. "Paperwork's tied up at City Hall. You know how that bureaucracy is."

Jones failed to acknowledge this universal truism. Rather, he grunted and nodded to his partner, who slid behind Coleman and began to slap handcuffs on him.

"What? You can't arrest me! What have I done wrong?" Coleman said. By this time, Hope had drifted back to base camp, although she hung at the perimeter to avoid incurring their wrath.

Where are those television cameras?

Coleman had heard about the mayor's new crackdown on street hustlers and panhandlers, but this was ridiculous.

"I ain't hurtin' nobody," Coleman said. "I'm just tryin' to save Mr. Bingle and preserve the memory of the man who gave him life."

"You're panhandling on city property without a permit," Officer Jones said, "and subject to arrest, fine, and jail time if convicted."

"Jail time?" Coleman turned to Hope for assistance. "Hope, please. You've got to do something. When are those television reporters gonna' get here? They're missin' the big story."

Officer Cruz turned to her. "You with him?"

At first, Hope looked around as if to say, "Who me?" But she quickly realized there was no escaping her obligation to help Coleman. She stepped forward timidly and flashed her press badge. "Sort of. I'm a reporter with the *Daily Doubloon*."

Officer Cruz sneered, as though she were yet another foe in his ongoing mission to clean up the streets of New Orleans.

The fracas had captured the attention of the Mr. Bingle fans, and they showered the policemen with boos and jeers. Looking on from the relative safety of the store's entry alcove, Fillmore didn't dare to venture into the fray. It was getting ugly quick.

He feared physical violence was not far off, and he didn't want to give these heathens a defenseless target for their anger. It would be like throwing raw meat to a pack of hungry lions.

"Hope, this ain't right," Coleman said. "You've got to do something. Please. Do something."

This she knew. But what? Hope flipped open her cell phone and tried to get one of her TV reporter friends on the line. Where were they?

Undeterred by the verbal slings and arrows, Cruz scooped up the collection basket and Coleman's presentation, while his partner whisked the perp into the back of their squad car. Without the slightest hint of delicacy, Cruz flung the materials into the car's trunk, making sure to dump the collected cash into a plastic evidence bag.

As quickly as they had swooped in, the policemen sped away, leaving a vacuum on the street in front of the store that was quickly filled by a news van. A young female reporter hopped out. From the other side of the vehicle, a burly cameraman materialized carrying his equipment.

"Where are they?" the reporter said to Hope.

"Where have you been? You were supposed to be here fifteen minutes ago."

"Oh I know," the reporter said. She was unmoved by the urgency in Hope's voice. "Councilman Jennings tried to touch his toes as part of the fitness program, and he passed out."

"Well, you just missed it. The police came and arrested Haywood Coleman for – can you believe this? – panhandling without a permit."

"Are you serious?" the reporter said.

"I mean, I know they're trying to clean up the city, but this is a little extreme."

"I seen it all, lady," a loud voice interrupted. It was Cheryl LaBorde, president of the Mr. Bingle Fan Club. "Dat poor man was just tryin' to raise money for a Mr. Bingle memorial, and dem police locked him up. Da real crime is what Fillmore's is doin' to Mr. Bingle. It ain't right."

From his safe haven, Fillmore could spot the signs of trouble. That LaBorde woman was a loose cannon. He had to step in quickly before the situation got out of hand. He bolted through the doors and went immediately to the side of the young reporter.

"I'm sorry, Willard Fillmore the Third, can I help you?" he said, flashing a greasy smile and shaking hands with the reporter. "There's been a lot of misinformation about our handling of the Mr. Bingle situation. I'd like a chance to go on record about our attempts to reconcile with…these people." He gestured toward LaBorde like he was shooing away a fly. "We've made every attempt at reasonable negotiations, but they simply will not meet us half-way."

Buying into Fillmore's claptrap hook line and sinker, the young reporter signaled to her cameraman. "Great. Joe, you set up over there and get us in a two-shot." She pushed LaBorde out of the picture. Without a second to spare, the camera went live, and Fillmore was spewing his propaganda across the airwaves.

Hope stood beside and watched, helpless. Inside her head, Coleman's words repeated in an infinite loop: *Do something.*

***

If any night could be called a good one to get thrown in jail, a Tuesday in late December was it.

New Orleans' First District Police Station, bordering the French Quarter and Central Business District, sees more than its fair share of action. But on this night, the main holding tank included only a smattering of small-time drug dealers, burglars, petty thieves, and drunks. This being three days before Christmas, an inordinate number of shoplifters also peopled the room, all of whom steadfastly proclaimed their innocence.

Those who might have posed any threat to Coleman kept a safe distance, interpreting his running conversation with an invisible entity to be the outward manifestations of mental illness.

Even the hardened criminals knew that, no matter what their size, you left the crazy ones alone. Coleman sat on a long metal bench resting his elbows on his knees. At varying intervals, he buried his head in his hands, then cast his eyes toward the ceiling. Venom laced through his words.

"I hate you," he said, his puffy eyes lifted heavenward. "I hate you I hate you I hate you."

He plunged his head down again and let loose a protracted groan. "Why?" A hand slid free in order to pound the bench in rhythm with his pleas. "Why why why why why?"

Coleman stood abruptly, almost bumping into a passing cellmate.

"Say, bra', whyn't you watch yo'self," the man said. Coleman looked past him like he didn't exist. He then turned and pressed his hands against the cinder block wall, addressing it as though talking to himself in a mirror.

"I don't understand. I've done what I'm supposed to do. And this is how you treat me. I give up. I can't take no more. You want me to help, you're gonna' have to meet me half way. I'm tired. Tired, you hear?"

Coleman spun around and collapsed onto the bench. "I quit, you hear. I give up. I can't do it no more. You want something done, you're gonna' have to take over from here. Leave me out of it." Coleman rocked forward and rested his head on his forearms, which were crossed atop his knees.

A crusty, old bum slid alongside Coleman. His stench preceded him. He leaned over and whispered something inaudible.

"What?" Coleman said, sitting up.

The vagrant smiled, his eyes but tiny slits.

"Be still," he said.

"What?" Coleman said, his impatience evident. "Get away from me, old man. You stink."

The rebuke did nothing to darken the man's spirits. Through the ferment in his brain, his smile grew even brighter, seeming to light up the room.

"I said, 'Be still…'" As he spoke, his volume went even lower. "…and know that I am…"

Coleman mouthed the final word silently, but it could not have thundered louder if it had been blasted from an amplifier.

Be still, and know that I am God.

Coleman reappraised his messenger, seeing in his soft eyes the countenance of an angel.

"Who are you?" Coleman said. He knew he recognized those eyes from somewhere. The man did not respond. He smiled again, and he slapped Coleman on the shoulder with his filthy hand. It felt good, so good. Coleman closed his eyes and swayed while the man caressed his shoulders, massaging away the tension and fatigue, soaking up the pain.

Coleman couldn't believe he was allowing a stranger to touch him, but he was unable to resist. It was the best he'd felt in days, weeks, years.

A warm vibration buzzed at the core of his being. Coleman lost track of time, listening to the silence. A vast expanse of perfect nothingness.

"Coleman?"

When he opened his eyes, he didn't know if it had been minutes or hours. The bum was gone, and standing in the doorway of the cell was the duty officer, ready to release him.

"Are you okay?" Berniece said, as soon as he emerged from the holding tank and entered the room where he would make bail. She hugged him tightly.

"I'm okay, I'm okay, baby," he said with resignation in his voice.

"I came as soon as Hope called."

"Where is she?"

"At the newspaper. Said something about working the graveyard shift."

"Hmm." Coleman mulled it over before proceeding to a new thought. "Say, 'Niece, I've been thinking. Maybe it is time to clean out

Reginald's room. You know, get on with our lives like you said."

Berniece looked at her husband, acknowledging the years of internal struggle that had yielded this result. How she loved and admired him. He deserved another hug.

During the short drive home, Coleman chose not to relate his experience with the vagrant. He did not quibble over the $185 bail, which wiped out most of his day's collection for the Eisenberg memorial. He didn't even try to make small talk with his wife.

Rather, he was obsessed with the idea of silence.

Be still, and know that I am…

Given her husband's difficult day, Berniece didn't begrudge him his quietude, especially because, inside her own head, her mind was racing with questions.

What had spurred Coleman's change of heart? Was Reginald trying to contact them from beyond the grave? If so, what was he trying to say? Had she even really seen his ghost, or had Coleman's dementia somehow spread to her? Was insanity contagious? What were the side-effects of Xanax, anyway? Where was this all going to end?

Berniece shook herself. Truly, she wanted to support her husband. Maybe he just needed the recent drama to break him out of his funk. Maybe a new job and new challenges would do him good.

Maybe it was time for her to toss the Xanax in the trash. Then again, as she looked over at Coleman, she couldn't help noticing that he was playing with a stuffed Mr. Bingle doll in his lap.

Maybe he *had* lost it.

The two rode in silence down Claiborne Avenue toward their Gentilly home, until traffic slowed to a halt at Elysian Fields Avenue.

"What the…?" Berniece said, craning her neck to find the source of the holdup. A half-block ahead, she could see a trio of police cars barricading the street while something resembling a semi-truck lay on its side in the middle of the lane.

Coleman looked up from the doll. "Can't you go around? Or turn onto a side street?"

"Honey, I'm blocked in," Berniece said. "I can't go nowhere."

Coleman couldn't make out the shape of the vehicle in the road, but he could tell that it wasn't a semi-truck. Without a word, he opened his door.

"Where are you going?" Berniece said.

"I'm gonna' go check it out," Coleman said.

"You ain't goin' nowhere. Just be still."

"What?" Her choice of words stunned Coleman. "What did you say?"

"You're like a little kid got ants in your pants. Whyn't you just *be still* and play with your doll?"

Be still.

Coleman set the doll aside.

"I'll be right back. Don't go anywhere." He

leapt from the car and skipped up the street.

"Haywood!" Berniece called out to no avail.

Coming upon the commotion, Coleman's hair stood on edge. Clogging the street was a half-finished Mardi Gras float, toppled on its side, having been towed by a pickup truck.

A handful of policemen gathered in the middle of the intersection, huddling around a man who scratched his head as if searching to explain the accident. Coleman could see the right rear axle of the float bent at an odd angle.

Truck must have taken the corner too fast.

The source of greatest debate, however, was the gigantic paper maché bust – mounted at the rear of the float – that had smashed on the asphalt.

With an early Mardi Gras just a few weeks away in February, preparations were already in high gear throughout the city, even amid the holidays. It was not uncommon to see floats in varying states of completion being shuttled from the manufacturer to a krewe's warehouse, where the finishing touches would be applied. It was a mundane occurrence, except, of course, when things like this happened.

"They're going to kill me," said the driver of the truck that had been towing the float.

"Aww, it ain't that bad," said one of the officers.

"But it was the King's float," the driver said.

"In that case, you've got problems," the officer

said. Coleman recognized the voice, and as he got closer, he could see it was Officer Duncan, who had apparently gotten a new police car after his previous one was destroyed. Duncan chuckled and jabbed one of his fellow officers in the arm. "Hey Pete, what's this mess remind you of?"

The officer shrugged. "Dat time da sugar tanker bust open on Tchoupitoulas Street?"

Duncan shook his head. "Think Thanksgiving."

The officer strained his memory. "A big freakin' turkey with a gimp leg?"

"No, no, no," Duncan said. "Well, it was the day after Thanksgiving, to be fair."

The officer's eyes lit up. "Ohhhh, Bingle."

"Bingo," Duncan said.

"Aw, yeah, dat was a mess," the officer said.

"Kinda' even looks like Bingle," Duncan said.

"No, it don't. It's Peter Pan," the officer said. "Ya see? It's written on da side of da float."

"Fairy Tales," the truck driver said, dejected. "That's our theme for this year. Fairy tales."

"King of the fairies," Duncan said.

"Who?" the officer said.

"Peter Pan," Duncan said.

"I thought dat was Little Richard."

"Little Richard ain't no king," Duncan said. "He's a queen."

Amid the debate, Coleman pulled closer and tapped the truck driver on the shoulder.

"Excuse me, sir?" Coleman said.

"Who are you?" the driver said.

"My name's Haywood Coleman. And I'd like to talk to you about your float."

"Yeah, what about it?"

"Well, I have an idea. I think I can help."

"Really?" The man's face brightened along with his mood. "Forgive me. My name's Thomas, Jimmy Thomas."

The two shook.

"Where's the Captain of your krewe?" Coleman said. "Is he around here?"

In every carnival organization, while the King changes annually, the Captain is the one who runs the show year-in year-out.

"You're lookin' at him," Thomas said. "Captain Jimmy Thomas, Krewe of Adonis."

"But why are you driving…"

"Listen, Mr. Coleman, between you and me, our krewe is so broke – what, with the economy and all – that I'm Captain, costume designer, driver, and garbage man. Now it looks like I'm about to go into the float-building business, too. So if you got any brilliant ideas, lay 'em on me, brother."

Coleman placed a hand on the man's shoulder and guided him away from the group of policemen. They looked over the shattered plaster spread across the asphalt. The Peter Pan bust was a mere shell of its former self and virtually unrecognizable.

"Tell me something, Jimmy," Coleman said. "What do you know about Mr. Bingle?"

Chapter 11

"Where'd you say this place was?" Berniece crawled down St. Claude Avenue in the Lower Ninth Ward, searching for the Heart & Sons Mardi Gras World Headquarters.

"You mean to tell me, you've lived here forty-five years, and you've never been to a Mardi Gras float barn? You never even went to one for a field trip in grammar school?"

Berniece glowered at her husband. "It's forty-four years. And no, I never went to no barn."

To New Orleanians like Berniece, Mardi Gras floats seemed to materialize out of thin air like butterflies from a cocoon, making those rare out-of-season run-ins on the street all the more special.

But to carnival insiders, the colorful floats that convey blue-blooded royalty come at great expense of time, money, and hard work from men like Troy Heart, whose teams of artisans spend the full twelve months crafting the mobile structures.

"There it is," Coleman said. "Turn here." He pointed to a massive warehouse that must have taken up an entire city block. It was painted deep yellow and trimmed in purple and green, the official colors of Mardi Gras, representing power, justice, and faith.

Two men stood conversing outside the building's unassuming Charbonnet Street entrance, while Berniece guided the car to a halt along the pothole-scarred street.

"Haywood, man, great news," said Jimmy Thomas upon seeing Coleman climb from the car. "The board voted unanimously to approve your proposal, especially since we didn't have any other options."

"Great, great," Coleman said.

Thomas grew serious. "But we'll need some help on the financing."

"I'm sure it can be worked out," Coleman said.

"How rude of me." Thomas turned to Berniece. "Jimmy Thomas, nice to meet you." They shook hands, and Berniece acknowledged the third man.

"Marcus, is that you?" She smiled wide at Marcus Butler and leaned in for a polite hug. "I haven't seen you since…when?"

"Since I took you to Alpha Kappa Alpha winter formal back in 1973," said Butler. He was a tall, lean, and handsome man with a clean-shaven head and blinding white smile. "And then 'Wood here stole you away from me." They all laughed.

Thomas patted Coleman on the shoulder. "Well, he's the man. If this plan works, he'll single-handedly save Mardi Gras for about two hundred and fifty guys."

"This is quite a year for you, Haywood," Butler said. "First, he calls me after Thanksgiving and says he wants to rebuild Mr. Bingle. Now he wants to save Christmas *and* Mardi Gras. 'Wood, you've outdone yourself.'"

"Let's not get ahead of ourselves here," Coleman said. He opened the glass door leading into the company's spartan administrative offices, which were a trifle to be endured in order to get to the heart of the business, the expansive warehouse studio where Mardi Gras floats came to life.

Butler led his party along the smooth, polished concrete floor to the center of the cavernous, sheet-metal structure. Floats extended as far as the eye could see in every direction, while the clamor of pounding, grinding, molding, and cutting filled the air, accompanied by the thick smell of paint.

"I guess there's no Christmas break for these guys," Berniece said.

"We're in the home stretch now," Butler said. "Only two weeks till Twelfth Night."

"Tell me about it," Thomas said.

Each year, the Mardi Gras season kicks off with the Twelfth Night Revelers' Ball, a mere twelve days after Christmas. While the date of Mardi Gras Day varies according to the Catholic Church calendar (officially, Mardi Gras falls forty-seven days before Easter), the opening of the season stands fixed and immovable.

"But I don't think it'll be a problem," Butler said. "Mister Heart was reading your story in the paper today. He's real impressed."

"Story?" Coleman said. He and Berniece exchanged curious looks. An older gentleman approached holding a coffee mug and a folded newspaper. He wore gray Sans-a-Belt slacks and a navy-blue nylon windbreaker that covered his round belly. His white hair was slicked back with Brylcream, giving his head a silvery sheen.

"This him?" the man said to Butler but pointing to Coleman. Butler nodded. "I must say, Mr. Coleman, I'm touched by what you're doing."

"Thank you, Mr. Heart," Coleman said.

"Call me Troy. When Butler here told me about your idea for the Mr. Bingle float, and then I read about your story in today's paper, I was so excited I couldn't contain myself."

"I'm sorry, Troy, did you say, 'today's paper'?" Coleman said. He motioned for the paper. "Can I see that?"

Coleman stared at the front-page story. The headline read:

SAVING MR. BINGLE

The subhead read:

Local man fights to preserve local Christmas icon, honor original puppeteer

The piece not only outlined Willard Fillmore III's systematic plot to eliminate Mr. Bingle and pin the blame on Coleman, but it also chronicled Coleman's failed attempt to make public the tragic story of Oscar Eisenberg and his forgotten legacy.

Coleman was almost as surprised by the byline: Hope Lawson.

Well, I'll be!

Troy Heart led his entourage to the battered shell of Thomas' float, where a crew of artisans worked at a frantic pace.

"I got my best team working on it," Heart said.

"I can't tell you how much we appreciate this," Jimmy Thomas said. "People think Mardi Gras krewes are a bunch of rich, old, white men, but we're just struggling to make ends meet. Mr. Heart, whatever it costs to fix it, we'll pay you back, no matter how long it takes."

Heart shook his head. "Don't even think about it," he said. "This one's on me."

"No really," Thomas said. Heart raised his hand to quell the debate.

"Let me tell you something," Heart said. "Do you know how me and my brother got started in this float-building business?"

He pointed to a fifteen-foot-tall figure at the rear of the float, fashioned from chicken-wire, with only the beginnings of its paper maché skin being applied. But from its rounded body and pointy head, you could already recognize the markings of Mr. Bingle.

"We were about fourteen years old and looking

for work. We didn't have no skills, but we lived down the street from this man who worked at Marigny Brothers. Emile Allen was his name. We used to call him Mr. Emile. We knew him 'cause he had a side job. He was the bug man, and he used to come to our house once a month to spray for roaches. Mr. Emile the Bug Man.

"Anyway, we asked him for a job, and he said the only thing he had available was a part-time gig making this giant doll out of paper maché for Christmas. I mean, we knew how to do that from art class and all, so we went down to his workshop in back of the Canal Street store. It was just him and this crazy little puppeteer named Oscar Eisenberg. What an odd pair."

His thoughts drifted off, but then he regained his direction.

"I tell you what, we had no idea he was talking about a thirty-foot Mr. Bingle doll, but that's what it was. They wanted to hang this giant doll in front of the store on Canal Street. Heck, my brother Phillip and I, we became famous. After that, it was such a hit, we figured, if we could do that, we could easily manage a Mardi Gras float or two. So that's what we did." He spread his arms to take in the scope of his enterprise. "The rest is history."

"Well, I'll be!" Coleman said, aloud this time for others to hear.

"I'm just glad this fit in with our theme this year," Thomas said.

"No more New Orleans a fairy tale than Mr. Bingle," Butler said.

"I tell you," Heart said. "When I seen that Bingle explode on Canal Street the day after Thanksgiving, it broke my heart."

"This way," Thomas said, "with Bingle as one of our signature floats, we can use him every year."

"And he'll live forever," Coleman said.

"Plenty people are gonna' turn out to see your parade this year, Mister Thomas," Berniece said.

"You ain't kidding," Thomas said. "This'll be a real shot in the arm for the organization. The Krewe of Adonis sure needs it."

Coleman looked down at the newspaper, marveling at the words on the page.

"You okay, 'Wood," Butler said.

"It's a miracle," Coleman whispered.

"What's that?" Heart said.

"It's a miracle," Coleman said, slightly louder.

"You're darn right it's a miracle," Thomas said.

"You'll get no argument from me," Heart said. "It was like the Lord answered my prayers. I ain't got no better explanation than that."

"Thanks again, Mr. Coleman," Thomas said.

"Seems there are plenty of miracles to go around," Berniece said. "Now we just need to find a new job for Haywood."

Heart looked around his compound. "Well, if you need work, I'm sure I can find something for you here. How are you with a paint gun?"

Everyone chuckled, but then a phone mounted on a nearby workbench began ringing.

"Will somebody answer that damn thing?" Heart said, finally shuffling to pick it up. "Hello? Yes. Why, yes, he is here. Sure, hold on a second."

A look of wonder in his eye, Heart held the phone out for Coleman. "It's for you."

Coleman reached for the receiver like it might be radioactive. "Hello?"

His eyes widened.

"Yes. Yes. Yes. Yes, sir. Yes, sir, I can do that. Yes, sir, I'll be there right away. Yes, sir. Thank you, sir. Thank you."

He handed the phone back to Heart. The blank stare on his face betrayed the ecstatic thoughts inside his head.

"Who was that?" Berniece said.

"Willard Fillmore."

"Oh, him," she said, her disgust evident.

"No," Coleman said. "Willard Fillmore the First. He just got in town. He wants to see me at the store right away."

Heart whistled in amazement.

"A miracle, indeed," Berniece said.

***

As soon as Coleman stepped foot in his old place of employ, he knew something was different: People were smiling.

He scanned the sales floor for an outward sign of change and locked eyes with Miss Jackson behind the Cosmetics Counter.

"Good morning, Mr. Coleman," she said, wearing a wide grin. "It's so good to see you." She dropped what she was doing, ran around the counter, and gave him a hug. "Merry Christmas."

"Merry Christmas to you, too, Miss Jackson," Coleman said, startled by the show of affection. "It's good to be back. Do you know where Mr. Willard is? He wants to see me."

Miss Jackson pulled away. "He does?" She sounded like she'd just won a trip to Hawaii. "I mean, yes, yes, I'm sure he does. I think he's upstairs."

"Thank you," Coleman said. He smoothed out his khaki, poplin jacket and headed to the escalator.

What's gotten into her?

He proceeded cautiously to the second floor, where he found Willard Fillmore I camped out in his grandson's office. Files cluttered the desk, and papers were strewn about, the telltale signs of a frantic search & seizure mission.

Coleman knocked on the door frame.

"Haywood!" Willard pushed himself up from the chair and moved as quickly as he could. "I'm so glad I was able to get a hold of you." He pulled Coleman into a bone-crushing bear hug. "We've really got our work cut out for us here."

"We?"

"Sit down, sit down," Willard said, sliding out a chair and returning to his place behind the desk.

"Is something wrong, sir?" Coleman said.

"Ha! You bet sweet bippy something's wrong." He leaned back in the chair, ran his palms over his eyes and up across his forehead. When he leaned forward again, the faint pink imprints gave him the look of a raccoon.

"But it's nothing we can't fix, I hope," he said with an easy grin. "That'll teach me to send in a boy to do a man's job." His smile disappeared, and he became gravely serious. "Look, Haywood, I want to personally apologize for the way my grandson has treated you, the insult and the disrespect. Had I known, well…oh, there are no excuses. I'm the boss here. I take full responsibility. I am truly, truly sorry. Truly sorry."

Coleman thought about telling Willard that apologies weren't necessary, but they were.

You're damn right you're sorry.

He felt the muscles in his face contracting, and he fought the urge to smile. Had to keep the pressure on. Besides, Coleman still didn't know where this was going.

"Do you realize how much this job meant to me?" Coleman said. "I put in twenty-five years at this store! That's twenty-five years of my life. And for some punk to come in and say, 'You don't matter. We don't need you no more.'"

A wave of anger swelled in Coleman's chest.

He balled his fist, leaned forward and pounded the desk. "This was my life, man! Firing me wasn't just no business decision. This was my life. This was personal. And to do it at Christmas?" He threw up his hands.

Willard knew he had no choice but to sit there and take it. He owed Haywood Coleman that much, so he nodded along slowly.

"I agree with you, Haywood. It was wrong. It was wrong, and I apologize. That boy…"

A commotion in the hall interrupted Willard's thought. It was the sound of female laughter.

Fillmore came into view in the doorway, or, rather, stumbled into view, accompanied by his three Playmates: Dancer, Prancer, and Vixen. His clothes were rumpled. His hair tousled. Eyes bleary. And the combination of cigarettes, alcohol, B.O., and vomit made him smell like a Bourbon Street saloon at last call.

"Uh-oh," Fillmore said.

"Uh-oh is right," Willard said. "Get your butt in here, boy. Now!"

Fillmore turned to his companions and shrugged. "Sorry, girls. Christmas party is over."

"Awww," they moaned.

"But I never got to sit in Santa's lap," Vixen said with genuine disappointment.

Prancer nudged her with an elbow. "Shh, can't you see he's about to get fired?"

"Heyyy," Fillmore said. "Easy now. Let's not

give the old man any ideas."

"If only I *could* fire him," Willard grumbled.

"Let's get out of here," Dancer said.

"Good call," Vixen said. She looked at Fillmore and gave a smile. "Well, it's been fun." They took turns pecking him on the cheek and disappeared, leaving the rogue manager to face his interrogators.

"This is going to be one doozy of a hangover," Fillmore muttered to himself.

"Have a seat," Willard said.

"No thanks, I'll stand," Fillmore said. That way, he could keep the room from spinning.

"Sit!" Willard said.

"Okay, okay." Fillmore collapsed into a chair beside Coleman, who regarded the man-child with utter revulsion.

"Man, you stink," Coleman said. Unlike Coleman's bedraggled, jail-cell cohort, Fillmore possessed no hint of nobility or wisdom.

Chastened by the remark, Fillmore tried to sit up straight. "Good to see you, too, Haywood. What are you doing here?"

Willard picked up a file folder and waved it at his grandson. "I think I should be asking you that question. When I walked into the store, I didn't even recognize the place. So many long faces. You'd have thought somebody stole Christmas."

"Somebody did," Coleman said.

"What's that?" Willard said.

Without a reply, Coleman raised his eyebrows

and threw his chin in Fillmore's direction. Willard cleared his throat and nodded, indicating that he understood the situation perfectly. He produced a newspaper from the pile on the desk and pointed to the story on the front page, which he held out for Fillmore to see.

"I would ask for an explanation for all this, but I'm afraid I'd just get more of the same lies you've been giving me all along."

Fillmore stiffened so quickly, you'd have thought someone had injected a steel rod into his rear and up through his spine. His mouth dropped open.

"Surprised, are we?" Willard said.

He tossed the paper on the desk and addressed Coleman. "When your friend, Miss Lawson, called me to get a quote for her story, it was the first I'd heard of any of this. Then she sent me copies of all these bogus documents. I swear to you, Haywood, this is *not* the way that Fillmore's does business."

"But Grandpa…," Fillmore said.

"Quiet, boy! I always knew you needed a good spanking. But no, your mother always insisted on giving you a 'time out.' Spare the rod, spoil the child, I say."

Willard sighed and rubbed his eyes again before continuing to lecture his grandson. "So then I call Mr. Alton Lafourcade at the newspaper, and he tells me about the strong-arm tactic you tried to pull. Despicable. It pains me to think that we're even of the same blood."

"But Grandpa, what about the numbers?"

Willard slammed his fist onto the desk. Any trace of the jolly old man was gone. "This isn't a numbers business. This is a people business. You treat your employees better than you treat your best customer. I see I've failed to impart that valuable lesson on you."

Willard sat back again and, as if taking in his surroundings for the first time, scowled in disapproval. "Ugh, this is a depressing office. Let's take a walk out on the floor. We can talk there. I'll be able to think a lot better."

With surprising agility, he sprung from his chair and led the entourage to the escalator and down to the first floor. As the trio descended, a murmur spread among the staff, and all eyes became riveted on them.

An older female clerk met Willard at the base of the moving staircase and shook his hand.

"Mr. Willard, I just wanted to personally thank you for the bonuses," she said.

Willard put his left hand over hers. "I'm the one who should be thanking you. Merry Christmas, Charlene," he said, reading her nametag and winking.

Another clerk whisked past. "Hey, Haywood," he called out. "Merry Christmas, Haywood."

"Hey, how you doin'?" Haywood said, waving.

Still another clerk approached, waving a yellow and pink triplicate form. "I got a quote on those thousand toys you wanted, Mr. Willard. The shipment can be here tomorrow if we place the order by 3 p.m. today."

"Do it," Willard said without hesitation.

"Yes, sir," the clerk said, excited.

"A thousand toys?" Fillmore said.

"For the Children's Christmas Party, which I'm reinstating, along with the Christmas bonuses that you canceled. I would get the honey-glazed hams, too, but it's too late." Willard thought for a moment. "Good God, Christmas chickens?"

"Hens," Fillmore said. "They're hens. Honey-glazed hens. And for the record, I heard they were quite tasty."

Willard glared. "We should've gotten hams."

"It's your money," Fillmore said, shaking his head in resignation.

"No, it's their money," Willard said, pointing his index finger at the staff scurrying about the store. "Without their hard work and dedication, I have nothing. And if I have nothing, then that means you, son, you have nothing."

He turned to Coleman and spoke as though his grandson were not present. "It's painfully obvious that this boy has a ways to go." Then to Fillmore: "If you ever hope to run this business, you're going to need to learn it from the ground up, starting at the company warehouse in Dallas."

Fillmore's ears pulled back along with his mouth, which contorted into a grimace of protest. "But, but, but I have an MBA."

Willard took this important bit of information into consideration. "Hmm, yes, well, I see your point. In that case, report to the Maintenance Department. I think our toilets could use a good scrubbing."

Again, he turned to Coleman, this time wearing a smirk. "In the meantime, I'll need someone to handle things here. Do you think you're up to it?"

"Are you serious?" Coleman said.

"Never more."

It was Coleman's turn to pull him in for a hug. The staff, who had all been milling about within earshot, burst into spontaneous applause. Coleman acknowledged them with a bashful wave.

The managerial procession started again toward the empty puppet stage. Drawing closer, Willard was alarmed to see two children race past them, shrieking in fear.

"Our next order of business is Mr. Bingle," he said. "I received the most disturbing letter from a Miss LaBorde. Come to think of it, Mr. Bingle was one of the main reasons I wanted to buy this store."

Willard stopped in his tracks and threw his arms in front of his colleagues to prevent further progress. "Dear God, what on earth is that hideous creature?"

At stage-side, a puppet hung from a hook.

"That's Johnny Winter," Fillmore said, clearly hurt by the remark.

"It looks like walking death." Willard inched closer to examine the specimen. "This is what you wasted five thousand dollars on?" Without waiting for a response, he barked out orders to his new Store Manager. "Haywood, we need to get Mr. Bingle back here quick. And we'll need to get the word out to the press. And we'll need to let the children know about the Christmas Party."

"Don't worry," Coleman said. "We have Hope on our side."

Willard smiled. "That we do. Oh, and another thing. We'll need to erect some kind of stage so we can disburse the gifts. Something big. I'm not sure we can do this indoors. There's going to be a thousand kids. It's going to be complete chaos. Haywood, do you think you can handle it?"

Coleman nodded.

"I've got just the thing in mind."

Chapter 12

There was no question the gods were going to cooperate when Coleman opened his eyes and saw the bright morning sunshine streaming in through his bedroom window. It was one of those beautiful, crisp December days that remind southerners why they live in the South. One day before Christmas, no less.

Later that evening the Cajuns would ignite their massive bonfires along the banks of the Mississippi, lighting the way for PaPa Noèl and his team of reindeer. And at midnight, in the hallowed St. Louis Cathedral, the Archbishop would celebrate mass, commemorating the birth of Jesus Christ. But before all that, Coleman had something more important in mind: a resurrection of sorts.

Watching the Mr. Bingle float roll out of the Heart & Sons warehouse, Coleman felt like a kid again. Pure, unadulterated joy swept over him, the likes of which he had not experienced, perhaps, since the birth of his son. Joy, coupled with wonder at the miracle that he had taken part in. He swore, once and for all, that doubt would never cloud his heart again.

"You gonna' take it easy this time, I hope," Coleman said to Jimmy Thomas, who sat atop a vintage John Deere tractor, pulling the float in tow.

"I don't think this old gal would do more than ten miles an hour if you tried," said Troy Heart, who patted the tractor lovingly as he directed it out of the building. Because of their ability to run at slow speeds over long distances, tractors were the vehicles of choice for pulling Mardi Gras floats. As Thomas had learned days earlier, pickup trucks posed unforeseen problems if, for example, a careless driver were to take a corner too fast.

"I don't care if it takes all day," Thomas said from the driver's seat. "We're getting there in one piece."

"Don't worry," Heart said. "We got Bingle cinched up tight with stabilizing rods running through his spine. He ain't goin' nowhere."

Coleman had to admire the craftsmanship of the float, which was accented by festive, red and green trim along its pedestal. The fifteen-foot-tall Mr. Bingle stood erect, with his ice-cream-cone hat just slightly askew in that playful way. His red-cherry eyes and licorice smile conveyed a familiar warmth despite their simplicity. And one of his little mitten-covered hands waved high in the air, bidding "Merry Christmas" to all, while the other clasped a three-foot-long candy cane.

Heart and his team of artists had employed their best handiwork to give Bingle's flesh the appearance of fluffiness from afar (although a closer inspection revealed a coarse, ropey texture). They'd even gone so far as to animate the figure, enabling his mitten to wave back and forth, just as the little puppet would do from his stage. At the same time, Bingle's green and red holly-leaf wings flapped gently on his back, creating the impression that he could achieve liftoff at any minute.

In the foreground of the float, Heart had allowed ample room for a rider to stand or, in this case, an ornate, gilded throne to be positioned. He produced a tiny stepladder and slid it in place so that Coleman could mount the float. Once he had tied the safety belt around his waist, Coleman gave the signal and the procession was underway.

It didn't take long for cars to begin swarming around the float, honking their horns, drivers and passengers waving, surrounding it on all sides like a presidential motorcade.

Coleman buzzed with excitement, as he surveyed the landscape unfolding before him along St. Claude Avenue. His face hurt from smiling so much.

In the distance, he could see men, women, and children sprinting across the neutral ground to get up close to the float as it passed by. He grinned and waved, greeting onlookers and exhorting them to follow along to Canal Street, all the while wishing he had some beads or other Mardi Gras throws to liven things up.

A line of cars, three lanes wide, formed behind Coleman. Drivers honked and shouted at the spectacular float. Mr. Bingle was an instant sensation. The tractor chugged onward, through Bywater, across Franklin Avenue, into Faubourg Marigny. Crossing Esplanade Avenue, Coleman caught first sight of the high-rise buildings along Canal Street, and his heart began thumping at an alarming rate. While his attention had been diverted toward the adoring throngs, two police cruisers had taken up positions at the front of the pack, lights flashing, sirens blaring, clearing a path through every stoplight until the float reached its ultimate destination.

At Canal Street, Coleman gasped in astonish-ment. The crowd packing the city's main thorough-fare – at one time the widest street in America – brought to mind the madness of Mardi Gras Day. Police barricades had blocked all traffic in front of Fillmore's, except for the procession of city buses that lined the center public-transit lanes, unloading hundreds of children and parents.

"Take it easy, J," Coleman called to his driver. "We're almost there now."

"Slow and steady, slow and steady," Thomas said, following his police escort onto Canal and driving the wrong way up the lake-bound side of the street.

The cruisers guided the float into position alongside the curb in front of the store, where a makeshift stage had been erected bearing hundreds, if not thousands, of wrapped gifts.

At the edge of the stage, waiting to greet Coleman and Mr. Bingle, was Willard, the unmitigated glee evident by the twinkle in his eye. He stepped carefully onto the float.

"Can you believe this, Haywood? Look at what you've done." He laughed and slapped Coleman on the shoulder.

"Me? I didn't do anything," Coleman said.

"Oh don't be so modest. Besides, there's no time to argue. We've got work to do."

"I hope you've got the permits for all this."

Willard winked. "Worth every penny."

Children and families packed the sidewalk and street, but with a few dozen steel barricades, the Fillmore's staff and the fine men and women of the New Orleans Police Department managed to maintain some semblance of order.

Like Disneyworld patrons awaiting their turn at Splash Mountain, eager children and their chaperones snaked their way through a maze leading to the stage where the Christmas gifts would be handed out.

A look of concern crossed Coleman's face. "Where's Santa Claus?"

"He'll be here in a minute," Willard said. "First things first." He nodded to Fillmore, who was

waiting on the stage. Fillmore scurried onto the
float, positioning a microphone stand in front of the
two men. While Willard adjusted the microphone,
Coleman scanned the setup. At the foot of the float
was a designated press area, where camera crews
had all set up their tripods. In the thick of the pack,
Coleman found Hope, jostling for position. He
squatted down and called her name until their eyes
met. She smiled.

"Thank you," he said.

"What?" Hope cupped her hand to her ear.

"Thank…you," Coleman said.

Hope shrugged. "Least I could do."

"Can you believe all this?"

"I sure can," Hope said. "You did it, Haywood.
Congratulations. You did it."

"*We* did it."

He reached down and held out his hand to lift
her onto the float.

"No thanks," she said. "I have a story to write."

"For the Obituary Desk?" he said, confused.

"Features," she said, "thanks to Mr. Willard."
Coleman glanced back at the old man, who was
tapping on the microphone to see if it was turned
on. Willard spotted the two of them and gave a
thumbs-up signal. "He had a talk with Alton
Lafourcade."

"Well, congratulations to you," Coleman said.
"You deserve it."

Coleman stood and turned to help Willard.

"Merry Christmas, Haywood," Hope called out from behind. He glanced back and smiled again.

"Merry Christmas to you. Merry Christmas."

"Testing one-two, testing one-two," Willard said into the microphone. His voice echoed throughout the canyon along Canal Street that was formed by asphalt, concrete, and steel. Willard beamed like a proud grandfather, truly relishing the spectacle playing out before him. "Merrrrry Christmas," he bellowed in his best imitation of a fat, happy Santa.

"Merrrrrrrrrrry Christmas," the crowed replied.

"Is everybody ready to come up and get a present from Santa Claus?" Willard shouted.

"Yeahhhhhhh," the children screamed.

"Santa will be here any minute now. But first, I have a very exciting announcement to make." The kids shuffled impatiently, wishing the old man would just get on with it. "Does everybody here love Mr. Bingle?"

The children roared. Coleman noticed a few of them hopping up and down in excitement.

"Does anybody want Mr. Bingle to come back before Christmas?"

More cheers, this time even louder.

"Well, I am happy to announce that Fillmore's Department Stores is not only bringing back Mr. Bingle to all its New Orleans stores, but Fillmore's is also bringing Mr. Bingle to every one of its stores throughout the country so children everywhere can share in the joy that he brings."

From the middle of the crowd, where they were waving their hand-crafted picket signs, Cheryl LaBorde and other members of the Mr. Bingle Fan Club erupted in cheers. They cast down their signs and wrapped one another in tearful hugs, celebrating their triumph as though their candidate had just won the presidential election.

Away from the microphone, Willard turned to Coleman. "Oh, and don't let me forget this," he said, reaching into his pocket and presenting his Store Manager with a folded slip of paper. Initially, all Coleman could make out was a number with a bunch of zeros behind it.

"What's this?" he said.

"For Oscar Eisenberg," Willard said. "Make sure nobody ever forgets."

Coleman held the check in his hands. Twenty thousand dollars could buy one heck of a tombstone and a plaque for every store. Coleman had seen checks for more money, but he knew the value of this one transcended the material realm. He looked down once again to make sure it was real, then looked up to the sky to make sure Eisenberg was watching.

Cutting through the clamor, he could hear the heavy thumping of a mechanical bird, which drew closer until it was hovering directly overhead. The deafening whir, coupled with the gale-force winds, sent the crowd to new heights of excitement.

Coleman searched the sky for other signs of trouble. All he found was a sturdy rope ladder that fell onto the float and a white-bearded figure in a red suit climbing downward to earth.

Even the assembled law enforcement officers seemed to find it amusing.

"Well, I'll be," Coleman said, smiling. Willard shrugged as if it were all a surprise to him. Coleman reached out to steady the ladder while Santa maneuvered down the final rungs and onto the float. Once safe, Santa shook Coleman's hand appreciatively. Coleman strained to make out his identity. Then Santa spoke.

"Excuse me sir," he said to Willard, "I'm going to need to see your permit for all this."

It was Officer Duncan, trying to look serious despite the red suit and bushy white beard. He broke into a grin and offered Willard a hearty handshake.

"I hope you guys are ready to give out some Christmas presents," Duncan said.

"Let's do it," Willard said.

Santa assumed his position on the throne, and Willard moved the microphone off to the side of the float, where he could bark out directions to the patient mob. Coleman took his place at the edge of the float, helping children across the short ramp leading from the stage. In no time, the team had achieved an orderly flow. That is, until a young boy approached the stage in a wheelchair.

Without hesitation, Coleman moved to his aid and reached down to collect him into his arms.

"Grab on," Coleman said to the boy, who couldn't have been more than nine or ten years old.

"Oh, thank you, sir," said a woman who looked to be the boy's grandmother.

The boy wrapped his arms around Coleman's neck, and Coleman slid his hands under the boy's back and twisted legs. He carried the boy to the stage and across the ramp onto the float.

"Now you be sure to tell Santa what you want," Coleman said, oblivious to the resonance of his words. He looked down into the boy's face, and his knees nearly gave out.

Staring back at him was Reginald, eyes aglow, looking fully at peace, smiling.

"I already got what I want, Daddy. I love you."

The boy then leaned forward and gave Coleman a peck on the cheek. It was all Coleman could do to guide him safely into Santa's arms without collapsing entirely. He leaned against Santa's chair to steady himself, staring all the while at the boy.

The flow of time paused just long enough for his spirit to get whatever little bit of healing it needed to press on with this life. Earthly life, that is. For his heart sang with the joy of knowing there was something more awaiting, something altogether different, better. Coleman cast his eyes upward.

Thank you.

When his attention came back down to earth, he looked out over the gathered throng and caught sight of an old man at the back of the crowd. He seemed to float effortlessly above the fray.

The man politely doffed his fedora. When he did, he revealed a balding head flecked with a few, errant gray locks. And those eyes, the soft eyes of an angel. He knew he recognized those eyes. Coleman smiled.

Eisenberg.

The old phantom reached out his hand and was joined by a young boy. Together, they turned and ascended into the ether. Coleman stood motionless, watching, clinging to the sensation pulsing through his body, the image seared into his memory.

"Haywood." He heard a voice, like someone trying to wake him from a deep sleep. "Haywood!"

Coleman looked down to see Santa Duncan lifting his special visitor from his lap.

"Oh right, sorry," Coleman said, scrambling to collect the boy, who proudly held a big gift-wrapped box in his arms. Coleman carried him back across the stage and down to his appreciative grandmother.

"Merry Christmas, ma'am," he said.

"Merry Christmas to you, sir," she said. "God bless you."

Coleman gave the boy one last pat on the head and watched him disappear into the crowd. As he prepared to receive Santa's next petitioner, he came face to face with Fillmore. Coleman sighed heavily and smiled the tired smile of a man who had already put in a hard day's work, even though it was still morning.

"I don't know 'bout you, Fillmore, but I'm beat. Think you can take over?" Ignoring the question, Fillmore stood agape, his limp finger pointing at the fleeting apparition in the distance.

"Haywood, did you see that man and...where did they...who was...?"

Coleman chuckled and gave Fillmore a knowing wink. "I won't tell anybody if you won't."

But Fillmore was having none of Coleman's jollity. He looked as though the fear of God had flooded into his heart, perhaps for the first time ever. He swallowed hard.

"Coleman?" Fillmore said.

"Yes, Fillmore."

"I've been such an idiot."

"Yes, you have. I'll give you that."

"I'm so sorry. Do you think you can ever find it in your heart to forgive me?"

Coleman thought for a second, watching Fillmore sweat. "Well, maybe on one condition."

"What's that? Anything. You name it."

"That you take over for me here and finish handing out presents to all these children. I'm afraid I'm gonna' collapse, I'm so tired."

Fillmore's eyes brightened, and he hugged Coleman like he'd just been given a death-row pardon. "Oh absolutely. I'll take care of it. You can count on me. Oh thank you, thank you, thank you."

"Besides, if it wasn't for your stupid ass, ain't all this wouldn't have happened," Coleman said. "Consider yourself forgiven."

Finally wrestling free, Coleman patted Fillmore on the shoulder and climbed down from the stage. Waiting at the foot of the steps was Berniece, who wrapped him in another hug.

"You done good, 'Wood," she said. "You done real good. I love you."

Coleman looked into his wife's eyes. She was the most beautiful woman in the world.

"I love you too, baby. Merry Christmas."

"Merry Christmas."

He put his arm around Berniece and turned away from the stage.

"Where we goin'? You still got five hundred kids who need presents. You can't leave yet."

Coleman waved off the protest. "They'll be alright. Fillmore's got it under control."

"Fillmore? Are you sure?"

Coleman nodded with the utmost certainty. "Yeah," he said. "It's time to go home."

Berniece started to resist, but the look of peace in Coleman's eyes thwarted her effort.

"Haywood," she said, the realization slowly washing over her, "you mean…?"

"Yes," he said, pulling her by the hand through the crowd. "It's time to go home."

About Mr. Bingle & Oscar Isentrout

The real Mr. Bingle came to life in 1948, when Emile Alline, a window decorator for Maison Blanche Department Store, recruited Edwin H. "Oscar" Isentrout to animate the puppet Alline had created. At the time, Isentrout had been working in a Bourbon Street burlesque club.

Isentrout performed four Mr. Bingle shows a day during the holiday season at his puppet theater in the Canal Street store. Mr. Bingle soon became a fixture on local television, appearing in commercials for Maison Blanche and in his own daily show, which ran from Thanksgiving to Christmas. Isentrout also brought his traveling show to other store locations as well as to hospitals, schools, orphanages, and anywhere else that could use a little holiday cheer.

A native of Brooklyn, New York, Isentrout worked with several touring puppet shows in New York and Canada before buying a bus ticket to New Orleans on a whim in 1947.

Isentrout never married, and he died in 1985 at the age of 61 after a long illness. With little money to his name and no family, Isentrout was buried in an unmarked grave in Hebrew's Rest #3 Cemetery.

Mr. Bingle, however, lives on to this day, thanks to Dillard's Inc., which purchased Maison Blanche in 1998, and continues to celebrate this unique New Orleans tradition every holiday season.